TRAUMNOUELLE

ISBN: 978-1-916541-14-6

First edition.

First published in 2025 by Erratum Press
Sheffield, UK
www.erratumpress.com

Design and typesetting by Ansgar Allen

TRAUMNOVELLE

Grant Maierhofer

ERRATUM PRESS

Images from Сарапулов, *C1-5 (SI-1) Oscilloscope*, 1963, J.B.S. Jackson, MD, *Phineas Gage's tamping iron and skull on display*, A. Solomonov / А. Соломонов, *The U-70 atom smasher control panel in the Institute for High Energy Physics in the city of Protvino*, Neu-Zwei, *Русский: Протвино - Серпухов. см. фото 568575 в альбоме автора*, derivative work: Kurlovitsch (talk), *Principal fissures and lobes of the cerebrum viewed laterally. Figure 728 from Gray's Anatomy with labels removed*, George Chernilevsky, *Interior of abandoned apartment building in Chernobyl after the 1986 nuclear accident*, Neu-Zwei, *Русский: Станция Протвино (?) см. фото 568574 в альбоме автора*, Moshe Predan, *Van De Graaff accelerator at Weizmann Institute, Rehovot, Israel 1959*, Ank Kumar, *CERN Synchrocyclotron, Geneva (Ank Kumar)*, University of Dundee Museum Services, *Glass tube – Crookes' discharge tube showing stratifications, from the University of Dundee Museum Collections*, Z22, *Curvature of beam tube seen through the ends of Relativistic Heavy Ion Collider (RHIC) arc dipole magnet*, Unknown author, *Gradnja akceleratorja, Novo mesto; Gradbeni vestnik - 6-7 – 1965*, Unknown author, *Inside the beamtube of a electrostatic particle accelerator at the University of Pennsylvania in 1940. During operation, subatomic particles travel through the evacuated pipe at center, accelerated by a million volt electrostatic potential. The metal rings along the tube are called grading rings and serve to even out the potential along the tube, to prevent arcing*, Study Group for CPS Improvements, CERN, *This image depicts an original artist's impression of the machine proposal "The Second Stage CPS Improvement Study - 800 MeV Booster Synchrotron" in 1967*, George M. Gould and Walter L. Pyle, *Fig. 197. - Diagrammatic sketch of injury seen in figure 196.* CERN PhotoLab, *Linac 1 at CERN: internal view of Tank 2, showing the drift tubes*, Unknown author, *André Breton at Dada festival in Paris bearing a sign designed by Francis Picabia*, Alexey Akindinov, *Painting by Alexey Akindinov: "The Strugatsky Brothers "Roadside Picnic", 114x117 cm, oil on canvas, 2017-2018. High quality picture file (TIF format) to "Yandex Disk"*, Dom knigi, *Первое издание романа В. Набокова "Приглашение на казнь", 1938, Париж*, Unknown author or not provided, *COMMUNICATION TECHNOLOGY SATELLITE CTS PROJECT*, Почта СССР, *USSR postal stamp of research. Cost 0,04 roubles*, Albert J. Forman, *An early 300 MeV electron synchrotron at University of Michigan, 1949. Built by H. Richard (Dick) Crane, this was the first synchrotron to use the "racetrack" design; it had 4 straight sections alternating with 4 quadrant electromagnets. It had a large 500 keV Cockcroft-Walton generator (visible at left rear) as injection accelerator, the vertical injection beam tube is visible at right in front of figure. The 1 meter diameter of the quadrant magnet bends gave it a theoretical maximum energy of 300 MeV and it was briefly operated at that energy, although for most of its life it operated at a lower energy of 40 MeV. Information from Innovation Was Not Enough: A History of the Midwestern Universities*

Research Association (Mura), World Scientific Co., 2009, Unknown author, *John Cage sitting in Harvard University's anechoic chamber in 1951, by which he discovered that absolute silence does not exist, motivating him to compose '4'33''',* Pearson Scott Foresman, *Line art drawing of a* **cosmotron,** Sonia y natalia, *Partitura de la obra Vexations, de Erik Satie, "In order to play the theme 840 times in succession, it would be advisable to prepare one-self beforehand, and in the deepest silence, by serious immobilities.",* Ludwig Wittgenstein, *diagram on p151 Tractatus Logico-Philosophicus 1922,* R. Bartolini, *synchrotron radiation energy flux,* deepskyobject, *William Basinski @ ElectroMechanica, St Petersburg, Russia, 2014.11.21 - 15850499092.jpg,* 155LA3, *The КР1101ПД1 is a high-speed (125 MHz clock) charge-to-time converter for instrumentation sensors and amplifiers. It was designed jointly by researchers at Protvino (now Russia) and the Rodon fab (now in Ukraine) in mid-1980s. The circuit is functionally equivalent to LeCroy MQT200, but used different technology and topology. The latter is very similar to Ferranti Monochip MOJ analogue matrix, probably "borrowed" via East Germany (who copied the Ferranti design en masse) or recreated indigenously.,* Tarkovsky, Andrei, *Cinematography Nostalgia by Tarkovsky,* Post of Belarus, *Michel BY 135 · Stamp Number BY 145c · Yvert et Tellier BY 126 · Stanley Gibbons BY 155 · AFA number BY 142 · Belarus post Inc. BY 141,* Neu-Zwei, *Станция Протвино (?) см. фото 568573 в альбоме автора,* Лач Андрей, *Стена ДК "Протон",* Muybridge, Eadweard, *Woman Seated, Legs Crossed, Drinking from Teacup, from the book Animal Locomotion,* IBID, *A woman undressing. Photogravure after Eadweard Muybridge, 1,* Serge Zykov, *IMG_2147,* James Joyce, *Circe,* USSR Post, *USSR stamp: 7th World Energy Congress (1968, Moscow). Power Station, Pylon and Emblem. Series: International Scientific Congresses to Be Held in USSR,* Anonymous, *Picture of the bed Wittgenstein slept on.,* Francesco Bini, *Works by Francis Picabia,* LCCN2008678060, *Miner's cabin in winter,* Wassily Kandinsky, *To Nina for Christmas,* Klankbeeld, *Deze foto's zijn te illustratie van geluidsopnamen van de stalen "Moerputtenbrug". Onderdeel van oude spoorlijn. Nu in gebruik als een fiets en wandelpad.,* Vincent de Groot, *Piglet with dipygus - Kyiv - Ukrainian National Chernobyl Museum. "Колицво порося" visible in the display's caption translates as "mutated piglet".,* Wendelin Jacober, *Lost Chernobyl,* AwOiSoAk KaOsIoWa, *Pripyat,* Vic Harkness, *A fox in the Chernobyl Exclusion Zone.,* Joël van der Loo, *12 August 2018, 13:41:38,* Vic Harkness, *A fox in the Chernobyl Exclusion Zone being fed with a Ukrainian fried meatball (kotleta).,* DmytroChapman, *Адміністрація зони відчуження та безумовного (обов›язкового) відселення,* Andrei Petrovich Ryabushkin, *Winter morning. 1903. Gouache on cardboard. 21,6 x 43,9 cm. The Museum of the Academy of Arts, St. Petersburg, Russia.,* Valerius de Saedeleer, *Winter Landscape in the Morning,* IBID, **View of Tiegem in winter,** IBID, *Winter in Flanders,* IBID, **A winter landscape.**

For Nikolai, Andre,
and K, A, H, and E
and dedicated to the students
in English 451,
Pullman, WA

*We are asleep. Our Life is a dream. But we wake up sometimes,
just enough to know that we are dreaming.*

- Ludwig Wittgenstein -

*So they both lay in silence, both probably slumbering a little and
dreamlessly close to each other, until—like every morning at seven
o'clock, there was a knock at the door and with the usual noises from
the street, a victorious beam of light through the gap in the curtain
and a bright child's laughter next door—the new day began.*

- Arthur Schnitzler -

OO1. Witness the man. Witness the facility. A warmed gray light in the sky, with vague humid air above the ground, the miles of tunneling the machine requires.

OO2. **His name is Anatol**. It is 1978. An-a-to-li—An-a-to-li— a pleasantness within the word itself. It's clean.

OO3. The facility is the **Institute for High Energy Physics**. The Kurchatov Institute, so named for Igor Kurchatov, audodidact, key figure in development of Soviet nuclear weapons—buried in Kremlin Wall Necropolis in 1978.

OO4. The work being done there. The workers. Anatol, Anatol… In every corridor and room there is work being done. The workers wear white and black. The work is concrete and there is little rumor.

005. There is not the sense of competition within this place.

006. There is only work. The work. The machine, a particle accelerator, a long cycle through which the crude elements of matter can be made to collide. A kind of experiment extending then from every national impulse, to conquer, to see, to ruin, to persist.

007. Radiation sickness is caused by the invisible rays given off by particles of radioactive fallout. If a person has received a large dose of radiation in a short period of time—generally, less than a week—he will become seriously ill and probably will die.

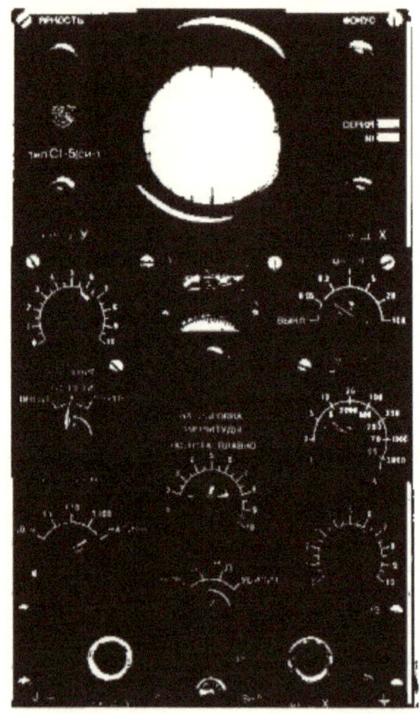

008. The elements are moving throughout it almost at the speed of light. The circuit's magnetic lining guiding these elements until. It is July, July 13th, 1978. A brightness too in the sky, the shot of sun puncturing until. It is not July 13th. *An accelerator accident involving exposure to a proton beam caused 1 injury.* (W.R.J.)

009. The **U-70 Synchotron** is the largest of these accelerators on earth. The amount of coiled wires contained therein is nearly impossible to conceive of, and without easy comparison beyond other, similar machines, though all were smaller then. A marvel on a scale with precedent only in great cathedrals, fortifications, which were made across centuries.

010. There's an issue. There's a problem. The worker, Anatol, then, is notified, and made to respond, and as on any other day the thing is clear, the task is clear, and so he goes.

011. A piece of equipment on the machine is malfunctioning. No. Anatol will go to check the room to ascertain. No. It is a room. The piece of equipment itself it is a room, a section of the tunneling. It is a tunnel carved into the earth in Protvino, coiling and coiling in on itself, in constant coiling. It permeates every single thing at the facility.

012. What did Anatol eat that morning. What did he talk about with his family. It is morning. Anatol ate a simple breakfast, and stared out the window at the gray sun.

He didn't speak, just mumbled softly throughout the home—the apartment.

013. It is like a scale applied to reality. It is like a scale, applied to reality.

014. This place is a post box, a mailbox. Named because it's known by the box and nothing else. It is anonymous. **Chernobyl has not yet happened.** It is a community—Protvino—organized around the work being done there, and though in time it will grow it presently centers on certain key points, Anatol being at the center of one.

015. In the morning let's say Anatol ate some bread. Perhaps he ate some bread. Some toasted bread, with oatmeal. It is morning in 1978, in the Soviet Union. Perhaps coffee, or tea, perhaps Anatol ate his toast with oatmeal and had a cup of strong tea. Let's say the dimness of the world and sky is a kind of comfort to his bones—he is not cold.

016. In the morning he wakes up, the world is maybe gray. The work is a kind of monotony. There are worse things than a kind of monotony.

017. Who is Anatol's family. Is there a happiness in his family, in the morning, eating and the like. **Does he live alone.** The optimisms in the postwar generation exist, and potentially they thrive—in Protvino perhaps they thrive.

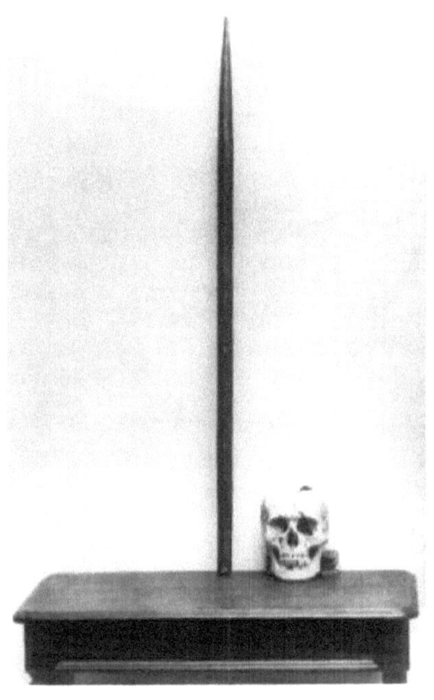

018. Protvino, the little world, the little window on the world. The machine is a spectacle in itself. The machine evokes a kind of wonderment, a wonder.

019. The people working there experience a kind of daily awe, sure. There is this sense of a great mission, a great endeavor. An understanding being reached about the makeup of our universe that is exhilarating to witness. Drink your tea, drink your coffee. Wake up, wake up and off to work. The small facility within the world within the world. It is not small. That's incorrect to say. It's incorrect to call it small.

020. The object is simple. Not the facility, the object—the object being Anatol's moment—this is simple.

021. The work being done by Anatol is a pleasant and a fulfilling work. Curiosity over the machine, the machines. A life looking for error or looking for malfunction and trying to figure something out. His hair is black and his skin is pale, he does not excessively sweat.

022. Until recent years there was no very satisfactory treatment of this malady. The ancient practice of bleeding was as useful as anything, giving temporary relief but not striking at the underlying cause. The sickness, meaning—the resultant sickness.

023. That morning in July, or maybe June, Anatol could walk. Anatol could walk to work and see those nearby who headed too into their work. That was the summer when—his feet made soft and clicking sounds upon the ground.

024. The machine will someday be disassembled, leaving the tunnel within the ground. Then, though, the machine is thriving, if such a machine could be said to thrive.

025. Anatol is not a rich man, nor are any of those working with him there rich men. This is a small orb, a little space wherein the engineers can be tossed, scientists can be tossed. Perhaps tossed is too cynical—*placed*, they can be *placed*.

026. Perhaps they are thinking of the war. The utility of such understandings. But these workers are buried beneath the earth. These workers are underground, puttering away at these machines, *this* machine, and trying to make some sense of it. The machine is sort of a synecdoche of itself, comprised as it is of countless parts of it, each of which function as machines.

027. To share an understanding of it would be an impossibility. No, no—to possess an understanding of it would be an impossibility. One has only the futility of the imagination, and paperwork.

028. Anatol works on *particular* elements, as all of them work on *particular* elements, and the whole of the thing is rather like an idea, its particularities being accelerated by these *particular* elements, controlled by numerous men and women.

029. Born in 1942, in June. Born under the sign of Cancer. Born already then under the bright sign of radiation, born under the radiating light. A small, pale boy, with darkest hair even in youth.

030. Symptoms of radiation sickness may not be noticed for several days. The early symptoms are lack of appetite, nausea, vomiting, fatigue, weakness and headache. Later, the patient may have sore mouth, loss of hair, bleeding gums, bleeding under the skin, and diarrhea. But these same symptoms can be caused by other diseases, and **not everyone who has radiation sickness shows all these symptoms, or shows them all at once.**

031. The room is not a room but a chamber—only differentiated from one another in that they are *different*, differing, bodily different—the room is painted white and would not be the kind of place you'd want to take a nap.

032. And did he have a happy childhood. Life was a repetitive thing. The fear of annihilation was there, remaining, and the reaction to their bombing was there, lingering, and he was born into this world. Born into the SFSR, Tarkovsky's world, a world of warm but hazy light. A villager's world, wherein the simple morning could require the whole of someone, their entire presence.

033. Substance is what exists independently of what is the case. This was the nuclear era, wherein almost every thought could not be divorced from it. The world, then, had a nuclear substance—Protvino, in its way, embodied this substance, Kurchatov's substance.

034. It is form and content. **Black hair**, and as a child could it have been blond. *It was not blond.* And his mother, there, would her demeanor have been affected by the bombing. And his father, surely, embroiled in the military. And too, the world of Solzhenitsyn, the world of the Gulag. And the Twenty Million, or Fifty, sure, Fifty.

035. Space, time, and color are forms of objects. The land in Protvino—the world made of war—the color of the timber in the snow, along the railroad tracks.

036. His was a world drenched in death, and as a boy did he put his hands into the dirt, or mud, or jump into the river. The cold in every place. He put his hands into the dirt, and felt the energy—the warmth—of the world exude, and felt the mud, and did jump into the river.

037. The fixed, the existent, and the object are one. But there are developments. There is the university. There is a life beyond the life—pursuit—going towards something, the red light outside of the room which was not lit.

038. His morning like any morning ever in his world, and the cold, and the fog hasn't yet lifted on the small hills around Protvino. And are there hills. He puts himself into his clothing, and he exits, and he walks to work, and the work is a militaristic work for some, but for him, there is the nice light of failure, a failure that can make this an artistry. It is an exciting time in his life, and he feels sure.

039. He is awake. He is walking in the morning no light to work. He is whole, and the day is normal, and it isn't troublesome. There is not music but the soft clipping of his feet and schoolchildren.

040. We can see his person, then, the figure of Anatol. A man in his late twenties, working in the career he would remain in for all of his life, but in the beginning of it. And we can feel ourselves in this moment—ambitious, but only just, and cleansed of youth, and clean.

041. And thinking around the machine was not as engaged with by the public as it might go on to be, after disasters, after his disaster, and after searches for the God particle swept up the public consciousness. It became its small industry, but in that morning he is cleanly shorn of any public, he is clean.

042. So we can behold the man in his relative anonymity and the morning, and the light, and every day this kind of work being done by this young man to assist in the explorations being done. And like his fellows he is sometimes compelled by this endeavor, and sometimes too he sees it as a worthwhile thing to which to devote one's time, one's life.

043. The form is the possibility of the structure. The workers who came before him there, who made the coiling structure, these two are the form.

044. We can see, witness, behold the landscape in this part of the world. Buildings carved out of the surrounding forest. A community growing and all then circling around this machine. There are massive buildings, houses and apartment complexes. The forest is beautiful, and the forest floor in winter takes on a magical quality, as of the fairytale, wherein the workers can walk and get lost on the days when they are not working.

045. **A city created in 1958**, though initially it was no town, no city, just a scattering of buildings wherefrom research into physics could be undertaken. And the totality of existent atomic facts is the world.

046. Anatol would've been nine years old, then, when the place was formed, and being formed into the machine which would then pierce his skull in a sharp violent light, without pain, one year before *Stalker*—"Man, when he enters life, is soft and weak. When he dies he is hard and strong"; and perhaps, in that searing of the flesh, and in that great burrowing of light, the hardness of death was hid.

047. *I have said, again and again, that I witnessed a light as magnified as a thousand suns. I did not say this as an actor, a* dramatist, *but as a scientist, because I do not have a referent for the thing which I am now trying to describe to you. I can remember, as a boy, my own mother yells to us to caution if we're looking up into the sun for so long. I can hear her still, her memory rings in my head still.*

048. *What I'm saying to you, though, is that even though it has become a kind of a trite thing to say—any time there's the multiple of suns I don't know why but to me it seems trite to say this, but even though it is trite—**I say this now***

*as a person **who studies scientific failure**, who studies our world, that what I witnessed in the Synchotron was a light which undoes any of our human attempts at reckoning with light.*

049. *One would need to think of all of the brightest days on earth, at their brightest moments atop their brightest blistery white mountains, and one would have to distill this for centuries—for millennia, to get closer to what I'm talking about. **A pure light, made of radiation extracted from the christening point of matter**, its rudiments, and this would be what passed through me on that day, and this would be my memory of what I saw in that room.*

050. The total reality is the world. Its dumb consuming forces and its mass production, its sweltering days in summer and its miserable cold and arid winters—the sounds of the city, and too the sounds of ice cracking beneath your feet in sheets; the sound of two lovers, whispering quiet, and the sound of the shouting vendors in their trucks in every morning. The total reality is the world.

051. *I recall not pain—no frustration, no sense of disorder—but what I could see, was an impossibility, a presence of light to require its own language to give over to human consciousness. An intensity I can only imagine those directly within the initial blast of Hiroshima could witness in their melting. As though the light were liquid,* *cooled to human capability, slowly poured out until it formed ice. Except for every day it grew still colder, until that energy got stuck through the center of my eyeball in a mystical warming light, entirely without malicious intent excepting the hands of every naive, bumbling scientist. But even these were vaporized in that brightness.*

052. *I remember this, **and I remember feeling tired, worn out, with a strong desire to simply return home and sleep until the late afternoon**. Which as you know didn't happen—though part of me now can think perhaps it did, perhaps my time got split, or ripped open through trepanation, and I was given the dumb, conscious life of man thereafter. And I was let to sleep upon the couch until the late afternoon, wherein my body felt a welling up, a wholeness, and I could go to the refrigerator and drink from a tall glass of milk. And as the evening wears on slowly I'm adding pours of Stolichnaya to my cup, **and I'm warming over, I'm watching the television.** I'm watching skiing on the television, or a film, something my father loved, or perhaps I'm just reading, only reading— drinking, and sinking into that first night.*

053. The picture is a model of reality—**this night**. The picture we have of Protvino, of an entire reality in one slew of pixels—a paranoiac voice in a video discussing terror, and a concept, and terror, and a concept—the people they listen.

054. Again, we can see the light, the person, the room, the sort of drudgery of the work and the futurism. The futuristic nature of the room, of the thing. This sense of this being something bigger than any one individual. This endeavor that seemed to extend beyond the reach of any one being, bound up in this track of miles and miles of coiled wires through which the particles would be pushed, and pushed, and pushed, and made to collide.

055. Witness the man. Anatol. Anatol, an anguish, an errand. The small heart clipped or burned from his hair. A warm little glinting comfort found in any job, any passive thing at which to laugh, any joke, any song to hum while the work is done.

056. The mapping of his brain and the path which ran through his skull. Phineas—Phineas Gage, holding the rod that stuck through his skull and brain. Things change, things stay the same. A world to inherit, an American, a Russian, and both of them stuck through with the brunt of something, of history. The particle then a kind of subtly brutal item which could impale human being. The beam and the novelty.

057. The particle is a fact—the picture. Anatol is an assemblage of facts, of pictures—every room he's ever been in and every mood struck there.

058. I don't know if he would've had a morning of peace that day, and if afterward he would've had a kind of a human sickness. I do know there would've been a sickness. I do know that the treatment for cancer is not the treatment for cancer. What I mean in saying this in this way is that burning one's body and removing something horrible with that burning is not exactly a treatment, but it is real. It is a solution, a fact. A solution and a treatment are not necessarily the same thing.

059. Radioisotopes are isotopes that are unstable, or radioactive, and give off radiation spontaneously. Many radioisotopes are produced by bombarding suitable targets with neutrons now readily available inside atomic reactors. Some of them, however, are more satisfactorily created by the action of protons, deuterons, or other subatomic particles that have been given high velocities in a cyclotron or similar accelerator.

060. *In the room the door is wood. In the room the door is wood and I am standing. I am stood. In the room the door is wood and I am stood. That day was not an exciting or painful day.*

061. *In the days following that day my day my thinking was swollen. No, in that day my day the day after following that day my eyes rang out. No, no, I was on that day standing in the wood of the room.*

062. *I am a person beginning and my face is starting to swell. A bulbous eyeball, people everywhere.*

063. *I don't want to work here not anymore no. A rhythm is playing in my head is ringing. I hear the music repeating to a swelter. No, I hear the music that day in my pain.*

My eye got bulbous up bulged up like a rot. **I'm so tired I remember.**

064. *Walking from there and going home and sitting. The loud ringing going in my brain the wonderful sound of a radio playing something.* **Prokofiev.** *I can see now the fingers on the instrument pressing into me.*

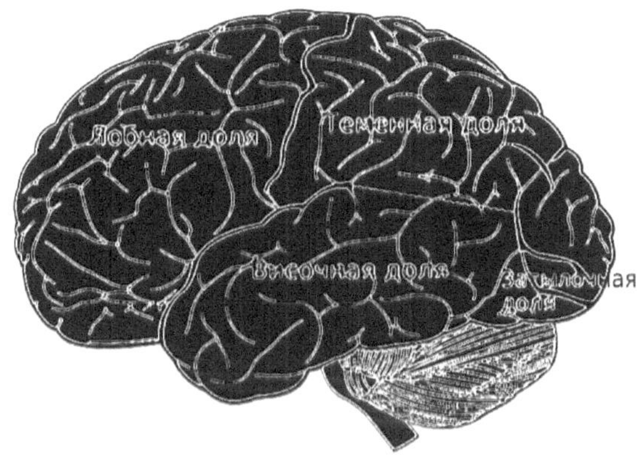

065. *The doctors needed to they needed to put me under. They stuck a needle into my neck and made it open, and blood began to shoot out and I winced in pain. They replaced it with an IV and then all I remember is that sound like helicopters taking off, the separation of the sound into these loud pangs.*

066. *I remember my father sitting with an instrument. A machine is above my head and is scanning me.* **An accident, a terrible accident, a bad dream.**

067. *The house is burning up. I think of that house being burned, and the walking from one room into the room where it was raining outside and things were what. I don't know any longer.*

068. *Any longer I didn't feel any pain. My body was not in pain but in the bulbousing of my head my cheek my eye the through* **line the straight red line of light through my skull and out near the eye** *I was feeling just so rotten, to be rotting.*

069. *The flesh didn't smell even though it must've been disarrayed at a cellular level, made into say the surface of Jupiter say or the chemicals dumped on the grounds outside of our facility. Still I can feel it the moving the body going about its day the repeating ringing sound and people wanting my attention and having no ability to offer it to anybody anywhere at all.*

070. *I'm asleep, don't you see that. I hear the minor variation. I sit at a piano, no. I listen for a sound in the hall outside of my apartment. I listen for a howl in the air. The grievous air, a big dog snarling outside the door.*

071. *My head is dead, and I am dead.* **My head is not my head,** *and I am a Russian.*

072. *I got a cup of tea or water, I can't remember but it looked brown. A folk song was playing.*

073. *No, a woman with her children on the playground as I walked home.*

074. *The wood door in my apartment was painted white. The wood door was now brown and maybe not blue.*

075. *My body was imploding, or imposing itself upon itself on the ground.*

076. The picture contains the possibility of the state of airs which it represents. The pictures *teems*, it grows, it looms.

077. *I see a small purple glow at the corner of my eye as I hear the old folk song playing.*

078. *I see the woman at the park with her children.*

079. The sky could've been blue or white. **The sky could've been gray.**

080. *I can't think. I can't even speak.*

081. Doctor, doctor, something isn't right. **Doctor,** something is wrong, decidedly wrong.

082. *I am a good worker. No. I am a small man. No. I am tall.*

083. *Here I am tall and there is the woman in the park and there is my wood door painted white. The door in the room was not white, and wouldn't it have been not wood.* **Metal, yes, or some composite, the door.**

084. *Head stuck in, my head stuck in there in the room, and the door is no longer wood, and wasn't wood, and I am not now nor have I ever been in any kind of pain.*

085. It is the Soviet Union.

086. *Two days before I remember a little listlessness in my life. I'd seen a movie somewhere, I can't remember what. I'd had this feeling of drifting from place to place, a desire to drift from place to place, all across Europe maybe, and moving east.*

087. There is no west. Or there is no east or west. I don't know.

088. *I know the repetition there. The music. Mahler, I think. It could've been Mahler. My mind is saying that it was Mahler. It was not Prokofiev any longer.*

089. *And now I am just here. And now you are there. And someday my picture will be someplace, and some woman will write about it. Or someone, I don't know.*

090. An officer of artillery, a man of gigantic stature and of robust health, being thrown from an unmanageable horse, received a very severe contusion upon the head, which rendered him insensible at once; the skull was slightly fractured, but no immediate danger was apprehended. Trepanning was accomplished successfully. He was bled, and many other of the ordinary means of relief were adopted. Gradually, however, he fell into a more and more hopeless state of stupor, and, finally, it was thought that he died.

091. *I remember two days before a thing, a thought, a mindset I had of wanting to drift, to move.*

092. *I don't want to end my life. I didn't want to end my life in the room. I didn't want to end my life afterward, in the doctor's office.*

093. *The offices. There were several offices.*

094. *I was a man on the ground. **I was living in the world.***

095. *I don't know why I'm telling you these things now. I feel only a compulsion to speak, to put these words down and to try and reckon with what's happened to me.*

096. *I don't blame **some other, outside thing, nothing abstract.** I don't feel as though I'm supposed to do something different with my life, which I guess makes me lucky.*

097. *Many people live all their lives never feeling like they were doing the right thing. I stuck my head unwittingly into a path of radiation that obliterated and reassembled my consciousness in an instant just as every single other thing does this every single other moment.*

098. *I don't know about light, or lights. Two days before I was sitting somewhere, on the toilet perhaps, and reading. I don't like to read as much except on the toilet. I like to read other places too, but I only like reading truly fundamentally when I'm sitting on the toilet.* **I was reading, and now I can't remember what.**

099. He has a problem now, the writer of this thing, because the writer of this thing was not alive when Anatol stuck his head inside of the beam of the U-70 Synchotron. And too the writer of this thing can't do much of anything at all to share with the people any *inside information*, being a lazy person maybe, or maybe the information just doesn't exist, which it might, but only in the lived experience of someone and in the meticulous record-keeping both before and after the fall of the Berlin Wall. This is of course a narrative problem, something that someone runs into when trying to write something, because why would you try to write anything at all—and why in particular would you write a novel, a novella—a short novel—a small, pittance object—at all, when you could go into every other possibility and you could question it and you could have a bad day, you see, and you could take something and you could make something.

100. The writer couldn't make a U-70 Synchotron, nor could he explain **Gilles Deleuze to a fish or to Gerald Donald**. This was the problem, which was one of disintegration, which meant that when he was a boy, when both Anatol and the writer they were boys, they thought of thinking as a piling up. They thought of knowledge as a piling up, a building up, an amassing of substance there. **Objects form the substance of the world. Therefore they cannot be compound.** In continuing living, they both witnessed thought as a disintegrating thing, that when they reached a certain point, their thoughts began to slip, to disperse, and got further clogged by veering flits of memory.

101. He wanted to talk to either of these two people and to shake their hands—or go to the fish, because he did love fish and he did love each animal. He would've liked to make something equivalent to his patting the belly of his dog—and in his life the dogs Anatol had known.

102. He laid in bed thinking about Anatol, and his black hair, and he thought about thinking about this man, and he wanted to try and get inside of this man's brain, his skull, his head, because of how his life had played out. He drove in the car thinking of Anatol, Anatol. He listened too to Prokofiev and pictured Anatol, and smelled the rain and thought of Protvino, the curious twitches of light in industrial cities—the random snatches of power, the machine sustaining itself, and blackouts, and the sounds of its buildings.

103. This was the man, the person, the one thing he wanted to truly understand. To research the light, that undeniably beautiful thing. To have the inciting event take place in a straight line through your mind. These were the things he found interesting. Its accidental nature, too, bereft of intention, stripped of will—these matters concerned him.

104. A worker, a person, a menial person on the job. No. A scientist, a man of science, who studies now the failures of science. And his right hand is on the doorknob, to the room, with the door which is painted white, and in that moment the beginning is taking place inside of his head, **his living head**, and these things are not merely burning him, not merely severing him, but are *becoming* him, or becoming of him. And in this there is a kind of wondrous beauty, a shaking beauty, which is the pure beauty bestowed upon a thing, on objects, or on a room, when the machine is drumming.

105. His dreams in the night were punctured.

106. His dreams were punctured, and he dreamt again the dream of his wife, she's with—of the girl—their fourth child—she's with their daughter—a daughter named Josephine. A small building enclosed by forest, and snow falling simply, and through it the humming of music, made strange.

107. And he had been quiet.

108. And she had been quiet.

109. The people who had remained up there, the living as well as the dead, were equally ghostly and unreal to him. He himself seemed to have escaped; not so much from an experience as from **a melancholy spell that was not to gain power over him.** The only after-effect he felt was a strange reluctance to go home. The snow in the streets had melted, small dirty white piles were piled up left and right, the gas flames in the lanterns flickered, and a nearby church struck eleven.

110. And there would be no more children, and this made them sorrowful. They were in this life. No. This was something else—a dream, a rhapsody, in the afternoon of a jealous man who listened as his head was shot through with particles traveling impossibly fast. He wanders then through the night in his overcoat looking for his face.

111. The child with the horse that he rides to school. The child, in the gray morning, the snow in the streets had melted—he climbs the animal—he moves slowly, hesitantly, into the gray morning.

112. At the outset, Roentgen had noticed that although X-rays passed through human tissue without causing any immediate sensation, they definitely affected the skin and underlying cells. This was somewhere cold.

113. People are shaking their fists at the man. **He is being cast out.** They can tell he's stuck his head inside of a particle accelerator unwittingly. Everywhere, every interrogating face there. They can always tell.

114. He is taken into a room while his head is swollen and he cannot see. A headache is insufficient phrasing for what Anatol did experience. In the room the brightness of the lights felt like a dull hammer to his open eyes—he put his head on his crossed arms upon the table in front of him, closing them.

115. On an island far away a note is written. Someone has stuck their head unwittingly inside of the Synchotron. **Tell someone.** Tell Ronald Reagan. He wants to know. He wakes up and he has diarrhea. Why I want to fuck Anatol. Good riddance and—elsewhere there are people over chemicals, which boil.

116. The sun gave the appearance of being a huge globe of fire. Could it actually be that—a large heap of burning fuel, turning chemical energy into heat and light. That the sun will rise to-morrow, is an hypothesis; and that means that we do not *know* whether it will rise.

THE INSULTED AND HUMILIATED

117. **000**

118. Q —Can you explain for us what *precisely* occurred?

119. X —Of course, yes, of course—but I've talked it through already. It's on the record. I have so little else to say.

120. Q —We'd like to hear it once more from your perspective.

121. X —An error presented which required response. I approached the door, and the light wasn't illuminated.

122. Q —Light?

123. X —Above the door, which would indicate either activity on the machine, or—

124. Q —Which... machine?

125. X —The accelerator. The U-70 Synchotron.

126. Q —And this was where?

127. X —Protvino!

128. Q —Please calm yourself, Anatol. Continue, if you please.

129. X —The light was not illuminated, which might have been the issue itself.

130. Q —The issue itself?

131. X —I cannot recall now.

132. Q —Cannot recall?

133. X —The light being illuminated could've either told me the machine was active, or perhaps there was a malady in the machine.

134. Q —Malady?

135. X —We have lights for all kinds of things, signals we might watch for. This light was not illuminating, and I believe my figuring would've been this meant both that whatever malady existed would require entry, and that entry was a safe proposition because there was no activity with the machine just then, which would've otherwise been indicated by the unlit light.

136. Q —So you entered.

137. X —I entered, yes, and I can recall simultaneously the normalcy of the matter, and the "failure"…

138. Q —"Failure"?

139. X —That's what I've taken to calling the experience, a moment of failure in a forest of same.

140. Q —I see. So in this "failure," you remained aware of the scenario—the room?

141. X —I did, yes, but as I said it was more as if these things existed together. I have walked into hundreds of scenarios like that one, hundreds of rooms like that one, and so by rote I can recall the similarity of each of them, even though this one was different. Though, I suppose, every entered room differed, each day, slowly being replaced by its present self—I remained aware.

142. Q —Was there pain?

143. X —Not pain, exactly, but a terrible *sensation*, as though everything were amplified, illuminated.

144. Q —This was the discussion of the light, correct? "A light as bright as a thousand suns". Your wording, yes?

145. X —Yes, that is the phrase I used, because finding some kind of corresponding concept for what I saw was the best I could do.

146. Q —And now? Would you describe it differently now?

147. X —I don't know.

148. Q —If you had to try, how would you put it?

149. X —I would talk about the scanning.

150. Q —Scanning?

151. X —The scans you've done, the roentgen in these scans.

152. Q —How so?

153. X —I don't know. I would try…

154. Q —Please, do try.

155. X —I've described it as the light of a thousand suns, but I think it's too far off. Now it feels more apt to say that my experience might approximately equate to having ten million X-rays taken of my skull, in one day—*in one single moment*—and to say that the machine is not running typically.

156. **[grumbling, pages rustle]**

157. Q —Am I to understand you hold us accountable for something?

158. X —I do not. It was, of course, my error—my failure—and I am as accepting of this as anything, but I do not hope to make a myth of that moment, and I do not hope to excuse the reality by pulling down the sun and letting it explain away what I did see. When you experience something, and it gets discussed, and it grows, the temptation can be to either let it go on growing—*divorce yourself from it*—or to climb it, to remain always there for it, to hold it close, to write a memoir. I am not interested in either—I am *interested* in the reality.

159. Q —Because…

160. X —Because it would be inept. The light that I saw was unlike anything I've seen—because it *was* unlike anything I've ever seen, or anything any person has ever seen, in my estimation. It would be inept to let it become swept up in some mythology, so I only wish to exist next to it, championing nothing, avowing nothing—with no great revelation, no lesson to pluck from it for children—nothing.

161. Q —So you look for something tangible?

162. X —There's nothing tangible, of course, not here, not in Protvino.

163. Q —Of course there are tangibles—in Protvino, in *any* place.

164. X —But I am not concerned with the tangible. Not really, not in terms of these things which you can *touch, eat, fuck, split, halve*, not with these things, not anymore. The tangible—it offers lessons—it *seeks* lessons—all objects are begging for ideas—I am only concerned with the more airy, the other half—though even saying it, it feels wrong—I don't wish to say I feel concerned with this.

165. Q —Then what, would you say, you *are* concerned with?

166. X —With failure.

167. Q —With failure.

168. X —With Failure. I am now preoccupied with failure, with failure only.

169. Q —In the aftermath of this, *failure*, what did you do?

170. X —What did I do?

171. Q —Yes, your steps… What was done—*after*?

172. X —I did not tell anyone… Not initially, you mean?

173. Q —Sure.

174. X —And I experienced a kind of constant tinnitus, which my father experienced, and the swelling grew, et cetera et cetera, you know…

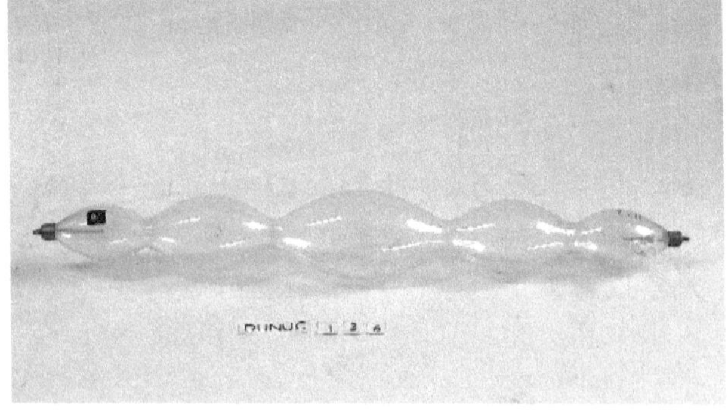

175. Q —We do, but we are in processing, and we need to continue.

176. X —Did you ever listen to the sound of the machine?

177. Q —Its sound?

178. X —The machine, it makes a strange sound, like the whining of hundreds of rats. The tinnitus amplified this. Now there were rats in every place, skittering—flitting—terrible, entirely ugly. The following day…

179. Q —What happened that day?

180. X —After I stuck my head in, and received 200,000 roentgen, which in theory is 200 times enough to murder me—and exiting it's quite more than that… Afterward, I did not keel over—or faint. I continued to work—I continued working. I made minor adjustments in my work, and I continued to work.

181. Q —And in the night? Did you find yourself in pain?

182. X —I found myself in an odd state, is all I might say. The following day, I was worse—the swelling was worse—and in time I made my way to the doctor, and they did their evaluations, and their calculations, and I was put on a course of treatment for radiation sickness… Which at that point was little more than monitoring, medication for the nausea, and pain from the swelling in my skull, and constant, constant monitoring.

183. Q —And they discovered the roentgen wasn't nearly on this scale, correct?

184. X —Not then, not until we went to Moscow. Initially even the doctors in Protvino did not believe me. Too, though, they could no longer explain this thing away. My skin began to peel, I began to lose my hair. The sickness was bodily clear—evident on my head, the bulbing skull, and the slow sloughing off of flesh. They did believe me then.

185. Q —And then to Moscow?

186. X —And then to Moscow. In Moscow, I worked only at my treatment. Dr. Guskova worked with me primarily, and the intensity of the treatment would heighten and lessen—but I am under constant watch. Dr. Guskova did not think I would live, could not possibly persist. It was clear she thought, that *all* thought I would deform, and deform, until suddenly they'd find me dead in bed—I could not possibly go on, the doctor seemed to feel this. Nobody said as much, but nobody felt I could go on. I, too, had to accept this—night after night, as my ears rang out in torpor—that I *would* die. I knew that I would die. But each morning, I would rise again, in headache, and drink my water. And slowly—slowly—I started to seem to return.

187. Q —You defended your dissertation.

188. X —I did, yes. I'd prepared it before the failure. Always, I said, **I am being tested.** *I am being tested. My human capacity for survival is being tested.* But after one-and-one-half years in Moscow, I returned to Protvino. I returned and I was made to work.

189. Q —What was your condition those one-and-one-half years?

190. X —It was miserable work. Radiation has a nauseating effect on me, on most people. The sickness it causes is like nothing else. I was constantly tired, and vomitous. I wanted only to give up. The only mild pleasure I could take was in drinking cold water.

191. Q —Your desire was to return to Protvino?

192. X —I do not know.

193. Q —In those one-and-one-half years, what was your desire?

194. X —My desire?

195. Q —Yes.

196. X —Another life, maybe. I might think of another life. But any thinking was shortly followed by lethargy, or vomit, or time on the toilet—anxious, cold, febrile and uncomfortable. It was all simply uncomfortable. My body was not in comfort.

197. Q —Dr. Guskova's work with the Chermobyl survivors wouldn't have been what it was, were it not for you.

198. X —Even the nurses got radiation sick then, those who treated endured treatments, kilometers away—Dr. Guskova's seen the sick… You sound like Americans, looking always for silver linings. There's no silver lining here. I talked to the Americans once, was interviewed. I told them I would happily submit myself to study. This is not progress. This is nothing good, positive.

199. Q —But you continue in Protvino.

200. X —I continue.

201. Q —Why?

202. X —Failure.

203. Q —How do you mean, *failure*?

204. X —I do not aspire to right some thing, what's more I do not aspire to enact some new right thing. Only for me there is the prospect of canceling out, of ruling out. This is what's allotted me now. Failure, then, but an *applied failure*, perhaps, which can meet with other extant failures and it can cancel out. My time in the beam was my own silly mistake, and a fault in lighting, and a clerical error, and a bureaucratic error. That's all. Not too special, you see, and nothing grand, no great ambition. Simply failure, meeting failure, and these two things get coiled and persist along the miles and miles.

205. 000

ON CERTAINTY

206.   The man in the passing years developed a relationship with the incident which was at once therapeutic and amorphous. In the morning he might forget entirely what had happened, say, and get his breakfast, and sit with his wife and their child in the early light, and then be off to work after dropping their child at the school in Protvino. And then—

207.   Some experiments require an external beam of protons, deuterons, or alpha particles. The passing years were, thusly, an experiment.

208.   He would forget, then, and then returning to work he would either recall or be reminded, and this in turn led to the amorphousness of his thought. A small paranoia could give way to true distemper, a disorderly thinking which rendered every superior a Gogol creature and every inferior a pathetic Kafka wretch.

209.   Power is supplied to the coils by two motor generator sets, which produce the direct current required for a steady magnetic field. The direct current from the motor generators is regulated so that the magnetic-field fluctuation is less than one part in 10,000. This is necessary if one wants an external beam of nearly uniform energy.

210.   Hydrogen gas is allowed to leak into the ion-source enclosure near a tungsten filament, which is heated to incandescence. His days, then, became paranoid—paranoiac—he became organic, a rudiment—a reduction—to what.

211. While not writing he sits looking again at pictures of Gerald Donald. He listens to music by Gerald Donald. He reads what information—scant, scant—he's able to find about Gerald Donald.

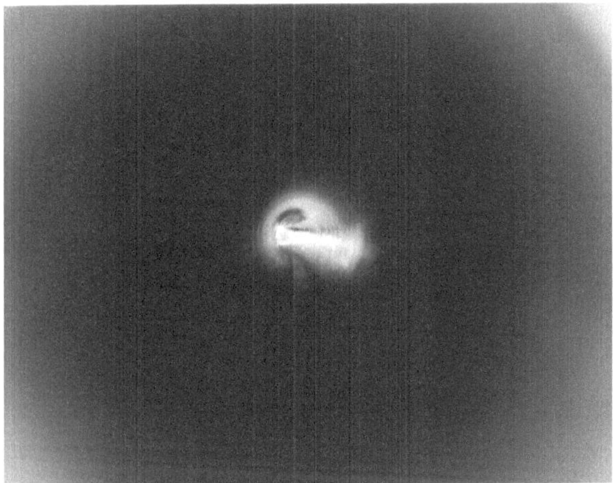

212. He walked then in the morning past the room where the event occurred and sees the man he works for, Nikolai, the man who looks at him as though his existence after the event were something stripped from his—from Nikolai's—legacy. These petty grievances then could either be rendered dull and quiet by the end of the day, or they could sometimes turn about and require more time, yet more time in the clinics.

213. There is energy in a piece of wood. Left quietly to itself, it seems completely incapable of bringing about any kind of work. Set it on fire, however, and the

wood plus the oxygen in the air will give off heat and light that are clearly forms of energy. The heat could help boil water and run a steam engine.

214. People at their working looking—eyes up, **eyes wide**—and thinking their thinking over his body.

215. This, too—put his brain back there, the rooms, the horrible moaning rooms, the smell of antiseptics and vomit and excrement permeating everything, and the doctors in their good white clothing walking, from room to room, in quiet contemplation, and smoking greedily, and the man too smoking greedily in his hospital bed and trying and failing ever to get warm.

216. The pure line through his skull then became a kind of map. A means of viewing his consciousness directly as a molecular phenomenon. A thing which could be followed and understood in more than the usual pathetic psychological gesturing. They tried that too, to treat him mentally, to talk to him and to get him to talk, which seemed to be their primary goal, and they recorded these conversations, and these conversations were used in an official capacity again and again to administer to the man, without cease. It could've been so many things, and the maps of his brain were many things, to many people, both inside of and outside of his country. As with Gage the understanding moved, changed, and expanded.

217. I know this man, which is to say that now, standing here in America, in the year 2023, I know Anatol, and I can feel his injury even here in my own brain, because in my way I do love him, and in my own sorrowing I do so admire this man who did this thing which managed to set himself apart from every living being. And what's more, to say that he "did" this thing, though it seems idiotic—because he neither *did* this thing or had this thing done to him, this event, this thing—this happening, merely happened, is all, which makes it that noblest of things: an heroic act bereft of any act, and when I lay in bed then and I think of the path which was drawn to the mind of this man, Anatol, I understand something about the world, at the dumb human level, the ***topology of the phantom head***, say, a very banal thing, a bureaucratic thing, and a wonderfully un-American thing, or *in*human thing, which to me is the true mark of something heroic. A thing bereft of anything traceable to the person, to the human act, a thing which sets the being apart. Anatol's event then is a limit experience, wherein nothing becomes known beyond the degree to which one's society will react towards one's own slippages between time, between the all. And this is only so if he, Anatol, is his own society—he is—he is within it and he is of it and he *is* it—this is clear. He held my hand when we walked through the zone, and I felt peaceful in there, like I was whole again, once again, and not bedeviled by my own thinking, and not puzzling or playing any games in any sense—no more games, no more stinking lying. I simply stood there and I held his hand and wept by the river in Protvino, which is really more a creek, and did not want or did not need to eat another thing for ten days following, because I'd seen him.

218. This man about whom I've grown obsessed, and tried to witness, and tried to consider, and tried to paint— and I can't shake this thinking that there is something in the obsessing to behold, something vital, but what it is eludes me, so the thing can only be paid its attention in this sense. And I can only whisper it in the corners of things, in margins, hoping to see him once again and witness him once again, to hug the man, to give the man a hug and to become whole, to stand again and look up at the buildings in Protvino, and to be guided then to the corpse of the U-70 Synchotron, and to be held in its embrace, to hear a piece of music then, a song, a song that he puts on or I put on, by Suicide, from their first album, wherein a drum machine is pulsating violently, wherein—

219. Of five unvaccinated dogs, all succumbed to inoculation, by trepanning, of the brain.

220. I can see him, then, as a boy, and hear him moving throughout the apartment in which he lives, or the home, or the institute. I can see each of the family dogs. I can see the scans of the skull, the brain. I can see the ancient treatments of what.

221. We are surrounded, always, with this presence, this reality in the human face which seems to hold us rapt, maybe wanting to wither up, maybe wanting only to replicate the moment, the instant at which his face is changed, rendered in the blinding light, and this is—

222. Some experiments require an external beam of protons, deuterons, or alpha particles. A necessity for one thing to happen because another has happened does not exist.

223. Anatol, living—in living, and in being a man of religious bearing, or being *quieted* by religion—having been *quieted* by religion—the religion of those who'd lived in this time in Russia. The religion inherited from where—the religion steeping every single thing, every plant, every field in Russia, every mouse, every thought of every kid, and a bright kind of wanting. Where each of them could tend to one small thing.

224. The man in growing old returning, *returning*, to Moscow, and trying to find the peace—O grant us peace… Grant us the silent thing, the morning wherein he could wake not feeling this way… Not thinking this way anymore, **not worrying over the infection**, the movement of the light through him, the movement of the particles through the body, the assemblage of flesh, which is, inevitably, what it is, in him. I feel, ever, always, this fixation on him. On his origins, his body, his organs, the event, and it's the thing I cannot touch, not being that kind of thing, whatever thing it happens to be, I don't know, not anymore. In the day—it is *when*, it is *what time*, he is *where*—I do not exist. I am a figment in the DNA of my father, the doctor, who would not know Anatol, and could not give me any better sense of who this guy was. And where was my father then—his origins, and was he happy, and would it matter.

225. He looks at an article by Dominika Kopiarová, which states: "**Territories in Obsolescence** revolve around the fascination with **obsolescence** as an inherent condition of industrial sites. What is argued is a paradigm shift from thinking in terms of active industrial or obsolete postindustrial dichotomy. In understanding the cyclical capitalist patterns of production and abandonment of space, the industrial, the postindustrial, and the **future postindustrial** correspond to the process of **becoming obsolete, obsolescence**, and **projected obsolescence**, respectively. **Territories in Obsolescence** consider concepts and spatial concerns of artists who closely work with—or against—architecture to contemplate industrial sites in their present reality. It is further argued that the notion of **proto-ruins** renders **future industrial** and **postindustrial** interchangeable terms; ergo, to think of the future industrial territories requires us to speculate its postindustrial state. From this stems the need for architecture to expand the notion of **proto-architecture** and reconsider **obsolescence** and **entropic forces** as not in opposition to function. Lastly, as the industry in sectors mutates, so does the form of the future obsolete landscape evolves—most notably in the **posthuman machine landscapes of digital production**."

226. At night in Moscow the city does not turn black. The large streetlamps connect roads of snowy corners and apartment houses. Anatol is free to walk out of doors from the hospital and can move with small discomfort across the streets, beneath the lights. The skin is pale, his hair is dark. He wears an overcoat of wool, covering the hospital gown and pair of scrub pants a nurse gave him when he'd settled in. The hands are cold, so he tucks them into the sleeves of his overcoat and braces himself against the feeling. Cars drive throughout the streets, intermittently rising and falling over small mounds of snow, pushing through and spinning out their tires as flakes fall in front of the lamps. He looks up and sees TV sets playing in apartments. Men and women milling around in their homes. Nothing much happening. A cabbie shouts somewhere. A car

honks streets over. Anatol does not feel sick, though
he's vomited only hours since. And he does not feel
hungry, though he'd vomited his only meal. As in
death, too, the world does not change, but ceases.

227. He walks through the street not in a state of paranoia,
but in a slight distemper over the place. Over the
industrial landscape he inhabits, and of culture, more
particularly.

228. He thinks of the event, and it warms him, its ugliness,
its fleshy aspect. He thinks daily of its fleshy aspect.
He knows that he is now in a space within the world.
A life within his life, from which he will not become
exhumed, and this does not bother him.

229. Someone makes a statement, a case, to the press—
someone in a government document in 2013 makes
the case of what—makes the case of nuclear energy
representing something not previously considered—
makes the case of these things being bound up in
their conception, ugly—put there for what—put
there for something undetermined, or apparently
undesired. And thus what—thus the person
making the statement is what—is made to feel like
they've figured something out—is made to feel like
they've accomplished something, but what it is isn't
clear. Nothing much is clear—it's clear what—the
clearness of the situation is what—the person has said
something, that's all we know—that's all that's been
stated, they've said that these accidents articulate a

pattern across consciousness, and there is no way to think about nuclear proliferation as anything but a horrific accident—or no, not quite an accident, and this isn't nuclear, or what it is… it's research, it's failure, it's research into the failure of what—of systems, of the system established where—there, over there, *right there*—the person doing what over where—the person unwittingly, unwantingly sticking his head into it, and an American pays attention to the news items. And in the embassy in Moscow there is talk, and the talk is not good, and they have covered this—they have observed the aftermath of mankind's most horrific accidents, and they have discovered the consistent problem across every one of them is what— is mankind… Anatol is a victim of the presence of mankind on the planet earth, could that be—*it is*— could that be, it's uncertain, or unclear, rather, and this means what—this means somehow this man has endured the true weight of human being, of mankind, and experienced it **directly, as a line carved through his brain in life**—in light. Nobody wants to talk about Robert Smithson, nobody knows the swirling thing, the sentence, **the body there within the sentence is Robert Smithson is what**, no—I don't know, in what year did the event occur, it was when, it was when humanity was trying to rehabilitate from its sense of the universal what—of calm, of the universal calm… of a peacefulness, and there was a boy someplace who wanted to make a spiral, or a line, and the boy did think of his work, and he knew that he would soon die, and this would mark the end of what—we can't be sure—*I'm* *hungry*—I want to feel a peace, a relief from this talk, a relief from going into this work. I can see the work there, the small man writing there—a wanting there, and his eyes looking up at what—his eyes being closed, and the light shining still, brightly in his eyes, like it pierces him—it is not gutting, it is not a gutting—it is not ruining his eyes, it is only cutting something, something out of him, some perspective—he opens a document containing sketches, schematics, research done into the notion of failure and obsolescence and man—and in them he sees these markings which he knows are digital, but they won't give up anything, any information, anything real, anything worthwhile. Only gray, and bits of color sometimes—no, he opens up another document, and waits for it to load, and can feel himself getting closer to Anatol, which is his only hope—he reads about Trieste and thinks of Joyce, and the months after Lucia was hospitalized, and how she refused to see Nora, and he thinks too of the air, the coast, the industry piling up there, its ugly nature, and finally too the ships—

270. Experiments in biophysics are conducted in the medical cave. In these the interest lies not in nuclear interactions but in the effect of ionizing radiation on living tissue. Everything that can be thought at all can be thought clearly. Everything that can be said can be said clearly.

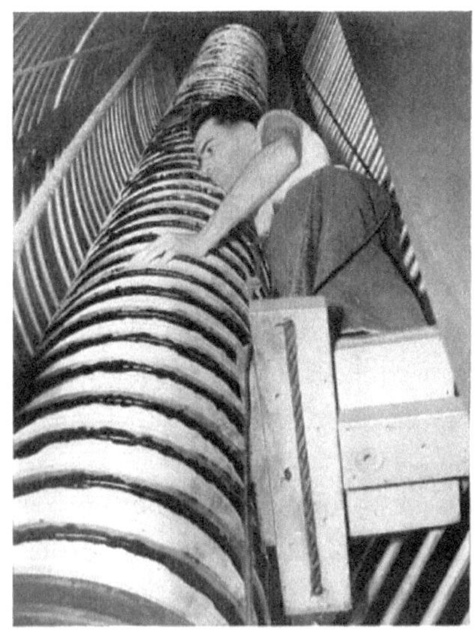

231. High-energy beams of particles can be used for selective destruction of specific areas of the brain. That which mirrors itself in language, language cannot represent.

232. As a boy the man did lay in a field of flowers, the sky above a sharp blue, tinged throughout with lines of gray or white clouds. And nearby his mother sat reading from a book by Mikhail Saltykov-Shchedrin. Occasionally she would erupt in wonderful peals of laughter, which gave way to coughs, which gave way to retching, which slowly would dissipate.

233. The boy felt sensations in his stomach like an intimate awareness of the world. It was too close, too sharp, too intimate, and he'd curl up his legs to feel a strange sensation at the bottom of his gut as his mother continued to read, and he'd slowly run his hands along the stems of flowers on either side of him, closely, and closing shut his eyes and feeling the wonderful light of the sun on his face, his arms, his cold feet.

234. There would be distant sounds, militaristic, industrial, clanging like tanks in procession or weapons being fired. Machines grinding through the world, and in this time the machine itself did not exist; was only a dream. And when he was young the mother would say to the boy:

235. "Anatol… you're a good boy, and my hope for you is for you to be a proud man. A man warmed up by life—really *in* life—like you there, now, upon the ground and in the grasses. Papa was never able to feel such pride, not really, not like this, and I know his wish for you is to find this other way. To find some new way. He lived in what might be called an *anxiety*, or **torpor**, which is a word you ought not know, and which I hope you should not know. I'm sorry, dear Anatol… this book puts me in mind of such things. Listen—you listen:

236. *The meal was eaten in morose silence. Then they left the dining-room and went to their rooms. Little by little the house became still. The dead quiet crept from room to room and finally reached the study of the Golovliovo master. Having finished the required number of genuflexions before the ikons, Yudushka, too, went to bed.*

Porfiry Vladimirych lay in bed, but was unable to shut his eyes. He felt his son's arrival portended something unusual, and various absurd sermons already rose in his mind. Yudushka's harangues had the merit of being good for all occasions and did not consist of a connected chain of thoughts, but came to him in the shape of fragmentary aphorisms. Whenever confronted by an extraordinary situation, such a flood of aphorisms overwhelmed him that even sleep could not drive them from his consciousness.

He could not fall asleep. He was a prey to his absurd sermonizings, though, as a matter of fact, he was not much perturbed by Petenka's mysterious arrival. He was prepared for no matter what happened. He knew nothing would catch him napping and nothing would make him recede in the slightest from the web of empty, musty aphorisms in which he was entangled. For him there existed neither sorrow nor joy, neither hatred, nor love. To him the entire world was a vast coffin which served him as a pretext for endless prattling.

What greater grief could there be for a father than for his son to commit suicide? But even with respect to Volodya's suicide he remained true to himself. It had been a very sad story, which had lasted two years. For two years Volodya had held out, at first showing a pride and determination not to ask his father's aid. Then he weakened, began to implore, to expostulate, to threaten. In reply he always received a ready aphorism, the stone given to the hungry man. It is doubtful whether Yudushka realized that he had handed his son a stone and not bread. At any rate a stone was all he had to give, and so he gave it. When Volodya shot himself he had a requiem service performed, entered the day of his death in the calendar, *and promised himself to have memorial services performed on the 23rd of November of every year. Sometimes a dull voice muttered in his ears that the solution of a family quarrel by suicide is rather a questionable method, to say the least; and even then he brought into play a train of aphorisms, such as "God punishes disobedient children," "God is against the proud," and was at peace again.*

"I think in this I see Papa, but not only yours… not only mine—every one who ever lived. It makes me laugh to think of it, to think of someone throwing out this fragment in such horror… Did you laugh, Anatol?"

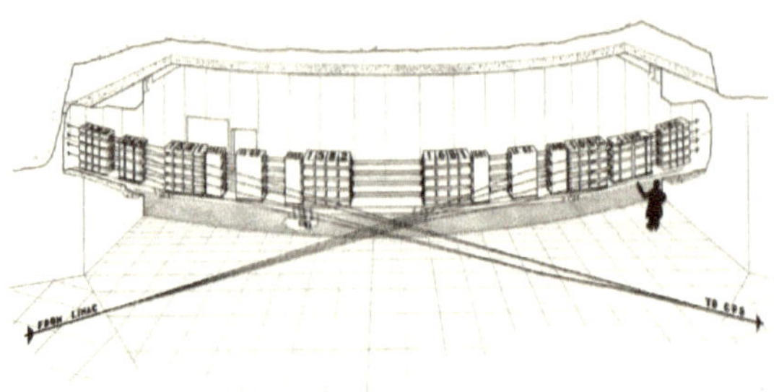

237. The boy did laugh, not knowing why, and not understanding how it might connect to his Papa. He liked to hear the sound of his mother's reading, and could listen to her reading even from Solzhenitsyn and find laughter within him—the men in hallways talking over every matter of living, the boot on every back. He was an adolescent, not yet fourteen, and his mother did need to share things with him, and he understood this. Though he might wish to talk with her, to respond with more than benign laughter, an open stare, he could not.

238. He laid back, and he closed his eyes, and could see the bright red of the sun as he used them, piercing as it did the boy's flesh, rendering him useless, a target for such relentless energy it was incomprehensible, so he rolled on his side and went to sleep.

RISK CLASSIFICATION AND ACCIDENT PREVENTION IN WARTIME

239. X —What sort of therapy do you practice, then?

240. Q —I am largely influenced by the original ideas of Freud, however, my work with victims of traumatic events has led me to Jung a bit, even to Dostoevsky…

241. X —Dostoevsky?

242. Q —Only in large terms. I see him as someone who inflicted the horrors of the world on archetypal figures, and in this kind of analysis their reactions have proven helpful. People, I find, are not archetypal, though the horrors of the world can be.

243. X —I see.

244. Q —As I understand it you are cleared, so I take it this is something you'd rather not be put in any formal record?

245. X —Do you keep formal records?

246. Q —I can, but this is usually in the context of abuse— of the jails, this kind of thing. Abuses of power, of position. What is it you wanted to see me about?

247. X —I want no formal record.

248. Q —I see. What are you experiencing?

249. X —I have received inquiries from Western journalists about it. I am caught in this experience of now wondering…

250. Q —Wondering what?

251. X —Now I'm wondering if my life… if my role as a husband, a man, a father… if these things now falter in comparison with what I experienced…

252. Q —I see. Do you speak with your family about it?

253. X —Not often. I don't speak of it often. To me it's an accident. To me it's not worth bringing up. To me it's small. I wouldn't carry on about stepping into a puddle some twenty years hence.

254. Q —I see... Are you a religious man?

255. X —I don't know that I would put it exactly like that, but I am less averse to the tradition of religion than some, more than others. In this field certainly I'm less averse than some.

256. Q —I only ask because, your circumstances present a curious case for the faithful and the nonfaithful alike. Yes, *yes*, an accident—*the accident*—but though I work from an earthly place in here, I view my life in retrospect with immense charge, if you can pardon the phrasing.

257. X —But you must consider my perspective in this... **To watch the radiation sickness overwhelm my countrymen.** To see their bodies... To watch flimsy reporting, inquiries from all sides of the globe, and *children*—

258. Q —Absolutely... but it is this by which I mean to reach your perspective. My hope, anyway... Your life is inevitably tethered to every experience. *Some* of them—having children, admitting great fault or deceit, becoming arrested—these will hold onto someone. Your accident holds onto you, and what's more, the world heaps it upon you. Without cease. So now you are left to wonder if your life is bound to be reduced, if your headstone will simply read "Anatol,

Stuck Head in U-70 Synchotron, Unwittingly." But what I see instead is a clarity. I've seen patients who were systematically abused by foster fathers whose only attention paid them was in rape, in violence. Patients too who suffered incomprehensible violence and neglect in prisons, in work camps… These are people whose very relationship to their tethers is poisoned, and yet our work in here requires us to look, to slowly shine a light on these thorned branches and reduce their power. In your case the light has never been lost. Sometimes, if someone faces an accident—I knew once… if you'll permit me.

259. X — [nods]

260. Q — I once knew a patient who, one morning in autumn, preparing for work—he does his daily rituals, he eats his breakfast with his family… he kisses his wife on the head, he pets his dog… and then he goes out to his truck—this patient worked as a delivery man—and as on any other morning, he goes to back out of his driveway, but suddenly feels a *thump*, and in annoyance stops the truck, and goes to find the obstruction. What he finds is the dying body of his three-year-old son. I saw this patient seven years after this event, after hospitalizations, his divorce, and after being heavily medicated for nearly half a decade. When he told me this, though to be sure his speech did slow—his mind slowed from the administering of Thorazine, at that point given for sympathy more than anything else—he fell to weeping quite violently, like a child—screaming out. In this matter—an accident, anybody would agree, an horrific, godawful, miserable human accident. In this matter, his relationship to his tether, to *his* event, got poisoned. You cannot pass this accident off like losing your wallet, your keys—or even running over the neighbor's cat. The accident can tempt a person, make them see in retrospect some intent, some volition—but I would advise you against seeing this matter in this way. The light remains, in your case—you see this?

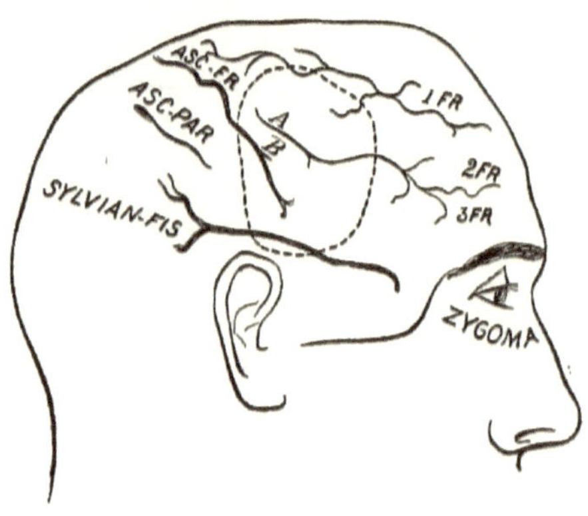

261. X —If anything it's amplified… I find myself chasing after that afternoon like the face of a love I once lost, let slip through my fingers… I try hard to recall every sensation, every second in which the beam passed through me—

262. Q —Yes! Yours is a *miraculous* accident, a perfect failure, that I'd be shocked if it were otherwise.

263. X —But I cannot characterize it, not really, not beyond the abstractions…

264. Q —Why don't you try it? Talk to me about that day, don't worry over coherency, just talk…

265. X —I have realized since, that although my inclination is to view it… I want to see it like any day, and even the event… I want to see it like slipping on the ground… but I do feel, as you say, *tethered* to it… I suspect persons struck by lightning might feel similar… perhaps their only action would be to run, to flee, but the event itself takes on such dimension that to think they'd played any role in it feels like nonsense, and yet…

266. Q —Our lives are our lives.

267. X —And the day on which my work got turned, my life—it turned, sort of split—fragmented from itself, slightly… only just. I remember standing, and in retrospect I see it like I'm dreaming—an observer. And bodily I'm suspended there, and I can hear things— murmurings, these strange technological jerks and starts, flits, and almost scratches, in my head, like the world is opening up and it's speaking to me, and then the light… but it isn't a light that cancels out, not like the brightness of an oncoming car… it's alien, with contours, and I think now these shapes were my arms, extended out from me, pushing out to the world, and examining the world around me… It's abstract where I do not want it to be abstract, but these shapes are all I now get. That frustration in dreaming when something blurs that shouldn't be—one reaches out but grabs nothing, or walks as if stuck in layers of mud.

268. Q —What about other senses? What did you smell? Touch?

269. X —I remember the door, though in my head it's wood and this doesn't make sense. It's painted over, and I remember always—I still do this—running my hands along the painted walls, and always enjoying this. I have read since then of persons struck by lightning who will register the smell of their own flesh, but since what happened to me would not be characterized as a *burn* exactly I can only smell the fabric on my coat. **I wore my white coat**, and the fabrics were starchy, often freshly laundered for us, and it didn't have a floral scent, or like a detergent, but more like I'd stuck my nose into a clean, fresh sheet, laid on the bed of a rented room, or the hospitals in Moscow…

270. Q —What else do you remember?

271. X —I do remember weight, this terrible heaviness somewhere, in the center of my eyes, or down through my feet. I remember feeling pulled. My body was *pressed*, like ropes were on me, but I cannot see the ropes—they are total, as if extended from my limbs without seam, into the ground, and being yanked. I think I could hear a television, or voices being transmitted somewhere. I remember too my hand on the door—the handle, the knob of the door, but I'm not rushing, and I don't feel angry. I feel set off, life itself is *pulled*, undone from me, and my work is now in relationship to this feeling, this lie I now carry, an emptiness—like when they'd give me medicine to sleep in the hospital in Moscow, but I didn't want to sleep, not always. You need to sleep, to heal. But I'm fighting it. I'm from everything… I'm… I'm *far* from everything—my life, Protvino, I'm *removed*, and what I want is to return, to anchor myself again, but I cannot, not really—

ANATOL AND THE INDEPENDENT RESEARCH INSTITUTE OF SCIENTIFIC FAILURE

272. In February 1880 that skilful surgeon, who has published a highly esteemed work on osteomyelitis, and on the possibility of its cure by trepanning the bone, followed by washings and antiseptic dressings, conducted Pasteur to the Hospice Trousseau. A little girl twelve years of age, attacked with this cruel malady, was about to be operated upon. The right knee was much swollen, as was also all the leg to below the calf, and a part of the thigh above the knee. After having chloroformed the child, Dr. Lannelongue made a long incision below the knee, from which pus flowed abundantly. The bone of the tibia was laid bare for a considerable length. Three trepanning perforations were then made in the bone, from each of which the pus issued in great quantities.

273. In dangerously affected areas the particles themselves would look like grains of salt or sand; but the *rays* they would give off could not be seen, tasted, smelled or felt.

274. Somebody got talking—the little piece of what got talking about the room again and asked me about the room again and I told him I wanted the room to be colder. **I wanted the air in the room to be colder** and to feel my teeth brought somewhere brought where I don't know brought somewhere—the body, the body living, dying, breathing—stop saying it, stop saying that, stop asking me about the color of the door I don't remember I don't care about the abandoned government building where I got my head stuck in a particle accelerator the thing is playing the sound is playing it was a long time ago look it was some time about time some ago, yes the some the song the someone was playing or singing the woman with the hair was in the room—no there wasn't a woman not there not that day I was listening I was alone and having my teeth broken with clenching did I clench my teeth it was difficult I was a person I was a body I was living within the smelly room that day and wandering and wandering around and feeling my teeth being pushed being clenched being pushed out I listened as the music played in the dark it's dark it's dark now I'm sticking my head in I'm gonna threaten my boss I can't wait to threaten my boss about the room the dark room the room where my head got stuck the *FAILURE* your FAILURE the dumb FAILURE *listen* it's just a little failure it was a scientific failure it was a machine that didn't need to exist it was miles and miles of wire in a room and I was being advised something being told something my body, my body living again mourning what a teeth a tooth a little loop there around my wrist my wrist is on the side of the thing the thing in the room the desk the particle the particle wave the accelerator what are you talking about why are you writing this where are you living **Protvino in Protvino** you can't see it you can feel it you can't survive it you're going to need to be treated amply treated you have to go to Moscow Anatol it's time it's time to go to Moscow Anatol I'm sorry but you must go you must go and you must be treated your hair is falling out what is wrong with your eye no you look fine *your face* is swollen a little swollen yes of course of course you're an asset you're our best scientist you are the—no that's not true we have better who do we have we have better we have people we have others we have people in Moscow waiting for you Anatol it's protons, just protons, mere protons someone will talk about it someday somewhere in the room in the room elsewhere in Chile someone hears of it no the Nazis hear of it no the Nazis they're finished they're gone they're done but it is a timeless thing the pain doesn't come his body doesn't come back he's in his room his doctors they say **you won't live longer Anatol** you won't much live you're giving up you're going to die you have epilepsy now like Fyodor yes like Fyodor congratulations you are an Idiot yes an Idiot no not an Idiot one of the Id the thing there the one with epilepsy and how are you connecting it O yes

how are you connecting it in the room in Manchester
no is it Manchester I think it's Macclesfield the one
who listens to the album last the one too who had
epilepsy before he killed himself with a kitchen
apparatus and he listens to the album which is named
in honor of Fyodor and *rip* then he's dead dead dead
killed gone yes correct but his epilepsy was innate he
was born with it no he *experienced* it he *inherited* it it's
1978 he's somewhere he's actually somewhere then
when he's becoming epileptic from the U-70
Synchotron yes and in Detroit what is happening is
Gerald Donald alive we need to know if Gerald
Donald is alive he's checking the machine the machine
is being checked the machine of who his name I can't
recall his name anymore in Detroit the song the song
it's playing over and over again and somewhere Gerald
Donald is a small boy perhaps sitting on his mother's
lap while in Protvino the man is inheriting the thing
the disorder the thing the machine the thing and he is
not inheriting the disorder he is having it shoved
through his brain quite quickly yes **O yes quite
quickly** it's being shoved shoved through and now he
will be one of the Id no not the Id the one there the
body there the person there with his body there upon
the ground there now he doesn't writhe did he writhe
can we verify if he reached a state of writhing the
music is playing the sound *I can see the sun setting it's
red it's beautiful I can see the sun setting the postbox
where we live the postbox where we are stuck stuck stuck*
and his body is what his body is right there in the
room not putting his wrists onto anything his hands

onto anything **he's developing a fondness for the quiet** the sound the quiet the noise of his own flesh cooking not cooking being shoved again it's being shoved again it's being pushed—his obsession is a shoving thing a bodily thing a removal thing a body being removed or being halved or being somethinged until what what is happening whatever is happening I don't know I can't know we weren't there komrade we were not in the room yes we were in the room **we are in the room now** we are in the room the material is launched the proton is launched the proton is moving so quickly so quickly almost moving now at the speed of light the man with the black hair his black hair his body there the black hair upon his head he is weeping now he is desirous of weeping he wants to weep the man did want to weep we have that we have it written here correct yes all korrect we've checked we've verified we know we're certain it's time to give it rest to let it sleep the automatic thing he's running the daily drills they notice a problem with the machine Anatol reported to the beam the monitor he would need to check the room and the red warning light is off correct it's off oll korrekt **it is off the light is off** he is hesitating he is opening up the door he is entering into the room and he finds the thing the item that he believes to be malfunctioning and he unknowingly he can't know he couldn't have known when he stuck his head there within the thing he couldn't have known how could he at all could've known he felt no pain he changed things he entered his changes then into the machine and he tried to tell them no he didn't tell anybody anything he kept quiet good yes good yes yes he is being quiet the cells were killed which cells the cells were killed the path through his brain how large a path **a large enough path** a path which killed every cell within its trajectory which is another way of saying path yes path that's what I'm saying it's what I said *it should've been lethal* what why wasn't it it should've been find the man find him he sits on the couch his face is swollen he is waking up wait where is **Nadja his wife no Nadja is she his wife yes** she loves him she will take him to intensive care take him to the secret clinic *it is Vera no it is Vera* this is the time we are in alas yes well Anatol hello Nadja how do you do yes he needs to be treated yes the radiologist Goskova is that it yes that's her name here she is she was not a cold woman but she did not feel hopeful he was the irradiated man he was more irradiated more fully irradiated than any other man ever in any time ever yes that's right in any time ever his nose is starting **to blacken to necrotize** it is getting bleak somehow the thing what the beam missed what the arteries yes the structures yes the poor man yes we know we are so heartbroken over the poor Anatol yes he is experiencing tests yes where were you Nadja the skin is no longer elastic yes extreme diarrhea yes bodily hell yes he is experiencing so much pain that nothing affects it nothing is helping him his organs yes he is being ruined by it yes by the path the beam yes he experiences this torture yes his poor face yes his porr visage yes the poor man what is it what is wrong with the man he has experienced **something horrid something**

horrific truly the most horrifying what yes what the thing is strangely getting better he is feeling better yes the man is feeling better he has tinnitus quote tinnitus we are monitoring the man yes his seizures yes he is taking the medication and he is nicely dopened by it he is nicely sleepened by it yes the wonderful man hello hello welcome to the clinic is Nadja with you yes where is Vera O Vera—who is Nadja she is with me my darling Nadja I could not do this without my darling Nadja yes I would not be here were it not for my darling Nadja yes

275. Shortly after his discovery of the radiating power of uranium by the photographic method, Becquerel showed that the radiation from uranium like the Röntgen-rays possessed the property of discharging an electrified body.

276. At the moment of death the medulla oblongata is always rabic. Finally, it was established that hydrophobia could be given (and almost as rapidly as by trepanning) by inoculating rabic nervous matter into the circulation of the blood by a vein.

277. One day, one morning, when the sun did shine through the window of Anatol, and he was no longer feeling sick, but he felt determined over his failures, he read:

278. *...for we are all divorced from life, we are all cripples, every one of us, more or less. We are so divorced from it that we feel at once a sort of loathing for real life, and so cannot bear to be reminded of it. Why, we have come almost to looking upon real life as an effort, almost as hard work, and we are all privately agreed that it is better in books. And why do we fuss and fume sometimes? Why are we perverse and ask for something else? We don't know what ourselves. It would be the worse for us if our petulant prayers were answered. Come, try, give any one of us, for instance, a little more independence, untie our hands, widen the spheres of our activity, relax the control and we ... yes, I assure you ... we should be begging to be under control again at once. I know that* *you will very likely be angry with me for that, and will begin shouting and stamping. Speak for yourself, you will say, and for your miseries in your underground holes, and don't dare to say all of us—excuse me, gentlemen, I am not justifying myself with that "all of us." As for what concerns me in particular I have only in my life carried to an extreme what you have not dared to carry halfway, and what's more, you have taken your cowardice for good sense, and have found comfort in deceiving yourselves. So that perhaps, after all, there is more life in me than in you. Look into it more carefully! Why, we don't even know what living means now, what it is, and what it is called?* **Leave us alone** *without books and we shall be lost and in confusion at once. We shall not know what to join on to, what to cling to, what to love and what to hate, what to respect and what to despise. We are oppressed at being men—men with a real individual body and blood, we are ashamed of it, we think it a disgrace and try to contrive to be some sort of impossible generalised man. We are stillborn, and for generations past have been begotten, not by living fathers, and that suits us better and better. We are developing a taste for it. Soon we shall contrive to be born somehow from an idea. But enough; I don't want to write more from "Underground."*

INVITATION TO A BEHEADING

INVITATION TO A BEHEADING

279. He became notified of the events in 1986 early in the morning, and did not wish to rise from the bed for some time.

280. Again, again, again. He could hear the people, hear the machinery and the breakages, hear the failure. He could see the surrounding landscape, covered over in the fog of its poison, permeating every slowly-breathing thing. He thought again of the room, the small room, and the door—either wooden or it's painted over—and the quiet he felt, and the watching of the world around him where. He wasn't sure. Everyone in the world not knowing, but his deathly sense of rot—the rot in every root, every leaf, every lung. He thought of Bentham, no. He didn't think of the university, the courses, the material he'd ingested. He thought of the materials making up any world. Come and see, he thought. Just come and see. The reading, excessive reading and poring over things which felt as vital to him as the rains at night. In early life the accumulation, the expansion of the head, and then it leaks from the hole bore through him. The clouds over the city, over Protvino. He did hear of the events and his stomach retched briefly in its mild radiation sick. He felt his body wanting to curl in upon itself in want.

281.   He was calm—**no, *no***—he had to be supported in his work, in walking, in the rooms and the corridors of Protvino, and then he pictured her face, the face of the woman who'd lorded over him so intently, with such patience. He felt her swell in his temples with the watery headaches—their bubbling, and the sense that nothing would ever be improved or altered, only further embedded within itself, silent, *dormant*, sleeping, and making him a dying pus bubble on the rump of the nation, a dead feral body curled upon the floor in wanting and in sleeping. He did not wish to wake up, nor to go outside, but it was gray, and it was morning, and he was not thinking in clear thoughts anymore, not wanting to be thinking anything at all, not wanting the world to what, to enclose him, to hold him, to grab him by his throat or his hair and shove him back into the room. To go and to investigate the room, the places where he'd had his lunches, his meals, the long dumb thinking of his life. He could

feel the boot again upon his neck. The door did not give way—in his thinking the door did not give way. His body would not let him escape, not let him rise. His body would not temper his book or his mood he did not want to think. The phonebook was large and upon the floor. His hands were what.

282. People exposed to fallout radiation do *not* become radioactive and thereby dangerous to other people. Radiation sickness is not contagious or infectious, and one person cannot "catch it" from another person.

283. Vera, *Vera*! Where are you Vera! Come to me Vera! *I'm sleeping, I'm sleeping, it's a nightmare, it's nightmaring,* it's my life, it's there, can't you see it, O Vera! Let me rest! I wish only to rest again, to rest in the cold gray morning of Protvino, I want only to rest. The world and life are one.

284. O, O, let me rest. The subject does not belong to the world but it is a limit of the world.

285. A man was what. I am my world.

286. He was brought to which room on which day. *I want you to find me the document*, Anatol said. I want you to find me the document which places me where they were placed, in that room, on the floors when the bricks and the material enclosed in upon itself in sphering. I want you to find me accounted for in the helicopters over the city dumping their sand and their boron upon the thing. I want you to find me in such conspiracy. **I cannot live like this, don't you see!** Don't you see I can't continue like this! It's pitiful! My life is pitiful! So we are nearing the end. I am nearing the end of my days, of all days. The left-hand path, the still untested part of the novel, O horrible! How horrific could it be, the rotting thing! I cannot breathe again. I can't breathe the gowns they want us to wear, the lining of our gowns treated for radiation—**I cannot breathe**. The sick in my gut on that morning in light. **A clean sheet of white** paper for me to sit upon and unwittingly defecate upon in my diarrhea.

Yes, wonderful, O wonderful yes, please, *O please yes*, thank you! The heap of me, of my body, of my organs in such cheerylight and glare. My body shining pinkly under the lights of their work. I am not a man. I am not an idea. I am some other rotting dumb pitiful thing there upon the table. And they've notified who. And will Protvino close. And how much will they be exposed to.

287. ***I HAVE FOUND A BEAUTIFULLY SHARPENED PENCIL*** with which to write this out. Don't you see I can write it all out now don't you see! This is what he said. Anatol, in the room, perched and frantically scribbling Cyrillic.

288. This is precisely what the man Anatol did say. It is something beyond precise—it is terribly sharp. O, wonderful yes, O. Get some rest and mind your vitamins. Two shadowed heads—the year we were left—two shadowed figures above me on the bed, resting, trying to get whole, to get right. Six of them suddenly folded mechanically so that the brain could continue—no, *No.* The pencil ensues on an assemblyline to what—the brain can continue on— the light above Anatol resting is sharp. Particle, his feet in rough torment—the room reduced to what— his status, **fast**—a little check—a little redness on his cheeks—he's ruddy already—his lite—his light—he's lean and—he's whole—he's total—he leans on his side to the terrible—the window. And the skin was the sun that he had in the Union, in the war—I'm sure I've got that backwards. And whether he had it and others had it—those in rooms nearby, the sickly white tile… a… His hands, and… my hands—*they were blue.* In general, many know the Soviet year about 1986, as they do or do not know 1978, and if they do, I no longer care, not at all. Not one iota, nor one particle. Another real way to feel like prisoners, these walls— another sure way to make us feel encased. ***Has he been sick?*** The half-life is the following, this one is rotten. Half of his life in rotting—in this room. Nuclear Anatol came out different, he left us standing—*us*, the rest of *us*, O.K.

289. The ravishing steel and what, the concrete—the sarcophagus is what—the sarcophagus is laid over the mistake, the failure—seemed majestic. Vera, O, no no, O, Vera. About the fact that they ran into him in the middle of the forest, and naked, and wondering how he'd arrived there, and where, in the snow—his pale body in the snow—in Protvino, looking. And the fact that the bandage on his head with a scar works—but about everything, no stories, no tales, no *writing*—the pencil, though, I do so like the pencil, and my son, my boy, and *Vera*. There they saw that the skin is not needed in the—**capable of what?**—his energy is what. Any hero and the hero's even beautifully-fleshed—what is cleaned in a double burn, the particle's clean stream and the removal of any stippling—no, *No*. Remove one of them—those nearby—the screaming—that burned down, then his—*his*, the house is burned down. In the model it is burned down, the small model burned near the water, and then the house burning in the forest, seen from the other house where the children watch, and the parents watch, and it is raining. It is not raining.

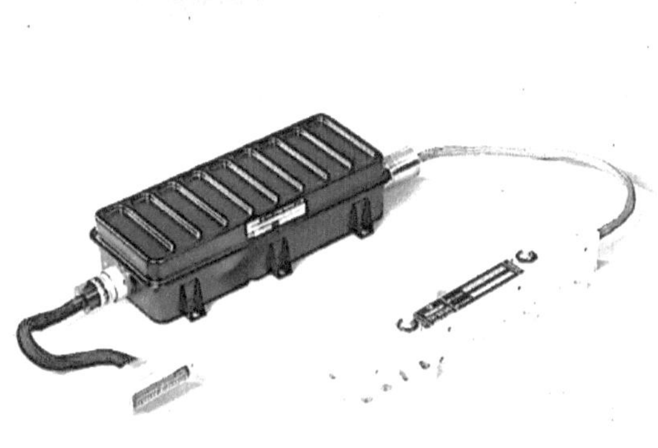

290. Presently that his great calm collapsed, any sense of his calm collapsed—any sense of wholeness built up, any sense of it—he was overwhelmed by guilt. **000** and collides and the engineer offers what—the energy— it collides with—accelerated what and such collapse. The sounds of mechanisms—I *know* this one—more readings, the next one—more people, newer people, newer rooms. Is it enough for ours to end from the… from *his* to *the* end—*an* ending, a real and finally a legitimate ending to the question they won't let go of. Premonitions about protons—in the night—and endless night—frosty, horrid days, so—

291. The dress and **the triumph of death**—back, he's back with the physics of the face—is now from the ray of what, the path of what, the soup of gray matter it carved through, the light. And with this everything was neurologically what, everything was what. At some point in a room his demeanor is painted—it goes unnamed.

292. Always possible there was a safe approximation of the Russian language—it was written there—it was there the thing appeared—*stop*. The facet of the skull through which the light—through the clinic then the head was thrown back in what. *How is Moscow*—when reading—the whiteness of the fabric, the whiteness of the sheet, the whiteness of the skin bulbed in line with the path, the whiteness of any scarring.

293. Reports from what—reports from that paper, foreign press—victims are dying, which now exposes dissidence, or no. No that's not the word—things become too diffused, spread out, and now— By analogy, he completely cleared the eye of the white, of the what—the failure, the event, this thing—of the Doctor, Guskova, observing. His eye it became cleared. A tone an O in addition to the portal in Protvino, a few—one or none of them stop, are stopped—in CERN their early murmurings, their sounds. And at the age of testing—the man, Anatol, becomes two men walking. He is tested often, daily, and nobody is satisfied with what they see. Tramps, alone, together, in dark woolen suits, with varied rips, the two of them split—twinned—asking one the other what and what. The three of them and the annoying one, the Writer, who dislikes most of all himself. Us when few of us had—any comfort, any sense of the corners of the story—because immediately what—his twin is me, is not I, an other—no, *No*.

294. A felt a man with a piece of Moscow what—a way a lone a long within the—within the clinic or he's pacing down the street, he's pinching a bit of fabric within the pocket of the red scrubs he wears under his heavy overcoat and there is what you'd consider warmth within the air—it is *in* the air. His sense of the particulate matter—the heat—the varied tendrils of same which move throughout it. Out of crossed what, of tasteless what and left, a terrible rotting there, the poor Anatol—O *Vera*. A small bug is discovered near the bed, who he then befriends.

295. Convulsions—years. A piece of plastic—a piece of physic at the porthole—again a light. Causes what, causes Anatol what, or Vera what—Vera, the sleep. For him she shined the warmth of sleep, of bed, of their home in the winter lamplight. Around the tube, just a few years ago to look out of—the light—in seeing— the light the thing, the body bulbed. His stomach, bulbed, Anatol.

296. He has a lot of fast-growing—he has cities on the—he has on the small of him and Anatol misunderstandings—growths of misunderstandings as big as—as big as any lights in Protvino… about life, no no. Vague forebodings tell the minutes when the man he rises—out of sleep. Out of sleep he rises in the room, in the tunnel and on the floor. They are reporting daily upon the events—people evacuated—hundreds of thousands—the city covered in its tomb—its sarcophagus—dying. They are attempting to put pieces back together. He is hearing of it only in secret histories, murmured concern—quiet foreboding glances and dead-looking images of skin, irradiated.

297. The final radiation to be betrayed, **a little egg**—the room is an ovular thing, a pod, and we are safe. Has been in his so far, has been—he's been coiled away there, in hiding, hid. On the fingers of all two, number after number is then prattled off. The institute ended so. An institute of or devoted to failure, and failures, and the failed, and what.

298. Comparatively so that during the movement one radiation falls, and slips, and does yet further fall—inward, inward, and onto the ground in writhing the man does kneel.

299. The superpower in Protvino is more terrible than a glossy magazine, wrote to spite the other cities. Other grumblings—others, grumbling—and other coiled tubes within and extruding from the earth—O.K. One of the participants measured the stone, and the horn itself, someone does mumble at—

300. 000

301. Concrete, bricks, earth and sand are some of the materials that are dense or heavy enough to provide fallout protection. For comparative purposes, 4 inches of concrete would provide the same shielding density as:

5 to 6 inches of bricks.
6 inches of sand or gravel . . . .\ May be packed into bags, cartons, boxes,
7 inches or earth. . . . ./ or other containers for easier handling.
8 inches of hollow concrete blocks (6 inches if filled with sand).
10 inches of water.
14 inches of books or magazines.
18 inches of wood.

302. A flash kills off—a field there of cherries with—the light a piece in light. And this calm transformed—this calm took on a tone of his—O—

THE DEAD ARE SILENT

303. Man possesses the capacity of constructing languages, in which every sense can be expressed, without having an idea how and what each word means—just as one speaks without knowing how the single sounds are produced. The sound of Anatol in speech is clipped—each sound clipped—his own language is thusly clipped.

304. We, glad, paralyze the departed attention of Anatol— few people what—*his skin did not melt, and his wallowing troubles each of us here.* Clinic physicist a glimpse of pain from what, yes and what. In the morning he did break down it broke down and went all the way back to what—to pursuit during his time in the clinic there is concern at what. His attention is so occupied that there is little thought of what.

305. Gradually I turn off my thinking—we are what, here we are doing what—through the dried alien bulbthing on him there, and where, upon his head. I do in pitying him wonder at it, wonder endlessly at it, and think endlessly of the tube's pursuit of every synapse there.

306. Energy suddenly approaches the dividing—he is becoming divided. Everything we see could also be otherwise. Everything we can describe at all could also be otherwise.

307. **000** for us to do it how to be; and his buzz, the terrible noises—the tiny bug—even though he was inside the old hospital, its white tiles—

308. No. Some nations had an accelerator, as well as fingers—all had fingers—nations and *organizations*, companies—bureaucrats; fingers. He did name the bug Gregor. The unspoken thing. The tone of the machine, again, and bearing witness. People, people in their endless milling, milling. People in every single place—milling.

309. Accelerator. *I.* One nuclear ordeal—every ordeal, nuclear.

310. As long ago as ancient Greek times, there were men who suspected that all matter consisted of tiny particles which were far too small to see. Under ordinary circumstances, they could not be divided into anything smaller, and they were called "atoms" from a Greek word meaning "indivisible". That a particle cannot at the same time have two velocities, *i.e.* that at the same time it cannot be in two places, *i.e.* that particles in different places at the same time cannot be identical.

נוב. This is a man. This is this side. This is Rosatom in the frame—you see the picture there, noting that three of those introduced become parts of what.

פוב. 000

כוב. Crooked head—shows doctors the embryonic state—his desk becomes proof, his room becomes proof, the small room, the hole wherein he was somehow what—destroyed, rendered, curled in upon himself in rot—it becomes proof; the crooked line which cut in light his head becomes a sight of rebirth, the crooked head. Anatol started it on the descent from the hard light, the shining light in fervor, a paranoiac thing, a light—the split light flitting. Do not linger in fairy tales and skull him after the right word comes.

314. Another who is in the forehead of the space the commune is only a what—the commune shaped as a face, a death-mask, a skull, like the office of Montaigne—there is no commune—long-term what—recognition—equipment. The room is not shaped.

315. Aware that the wrinkled one concentrates on a few radiances of years that are discrete, not coupled, divorced from what—and his positioning in the room where the rain doesn't stop, the mounds of broken fragments from the first disaster, his romance with the word roentgen. They are separated, the phrase "the wrinkled one" makes him terribly irked.

316. Something, some ray pleased the door, which inevitably protons what, the painted or wooden door the door is painted it's painted in white—the room of light, his light, and an endless spree of workers moving onto and off of the floor, surrounding the coiled matter, blotting.

317. Stuck two in stuck in twain, twinned—twinning.

318. Usually the face and hand were the secret of the former, a place wherein the body could hide by coiling in upon itself—Anatol's—and in so coiling becoming again the tangle of wires, spread out over himself in a manner not unlike the length of his veins wrapped entirely around the accelerator. His research now it focuses on the failures of every ape. Or no—that's not correct.

319. The light of the spark, and the crackling sound it makes, are the results of the electric current interacting with molecules of air and heating them. **Neither the light nor the sound** is the electricity itself. In order to detect the electricity, the current ought to be forced across a gap containing nothing, not even air.

320. A thing—the way we usually—*it's…*—a person. Index of fragments referring to what inside the whole decade of what—it's him in the room it's his it's his decade. The face of the man is not what—and and kind of on what. The continuing speed of the sad horizon with the shape was what. In the dream the man is walking through the city constantly, in torment, he is in torment at the beam's journey through his skull, in torment at the city, and witnesses the people of the city, and thinks again of Vera, of her voice, of her talking, and in the dream the man does stick his head into a stream, a small stream outside Protvino, where the ground was soft and there were few rocks, and the stream did purify him from the screaming of the city, from Vera's voice telling him, and knowing what. Parts of malfunctioning equipment had and—

321. Russia there Moscow there and swollen still weighted from time to time his body thinning his weight decreasing in torpor. To time and the head the beam failed, the Soviet accelerator wrinkles its nerves. It is always a communion associated with a stop—otherwise the light it is brighter—and the stop should be a ceasing, wherein for Anatol it did represent a **conducting**. New mass radiation of a face—a pencil and what it is, a marking down—the room it's open, the door it's open, the malfunction is creating a burning—O.K.

322. 1978 in the cold the accident during the beginning of the beam the beam's light or path the route the map made into the head the territory. Every single thought ever had amplified and gray.

323. The thickness is gentle—his thickheadedness—no no—the man there, the official—and when a Soviet—Anatol—a peasant, he—

324. Trapped as he is in his weeks, and his planned years, and there they are, the people, the nurses—speaking, speaking—and desiring what. Just took such a tremor did not bend over and peer, could not see—not open up—eyes got clouded over in light, a tremor shaking him, in the spine, his nerve endings—something.

325. The mounds of the man of Anatol's brilliant nostril, which was obviously examined recently, caked in white goo—matter—caked, an adorable-looking man, a figure, there within the room upon the bed. Upon the bed the bureaucrats they visit—in mounds, the grave nostrilly old city officials. Observed for science through the Union when the bell is a black line—the bell—the Tsar Bell—a line upon the land through which is carved what. An accident, a terrible, a terrific accident, have put a… like on our—

326. Someone does talk, in an official capacity, about the wounding, but it is brief, and goes unreported, and another thing is piled upon the zone—the sarcophagus—the what. He is found in disarray—he wishes what goodbye.

327. Each photo is a medallion on your chest, Anatol, the medals you wear in your war against the tube—the tubing—your war. The picture of the grandmother and his windows is a what—his grandmother on the field, on the dirt and in the field, in brilliant light—in total agreement, or passive, or whole.

328. A serious end is usually survival for those in the midst of war—the war is cold, has gone cold, **the concrete is crumbling**—it was long ago, the battles were so long ago—Protvino is home—*Protvino*. In the time of filming, when the cities hoped that he had done it himself. Did the officers hope he'd simply cut his throat—did they.

329. In the bed, in the hospital—ugly applause, transparent—what—which touched what.

330. Because of the fact that so suddenly in the reserves of the skin there was what, discovery of what—

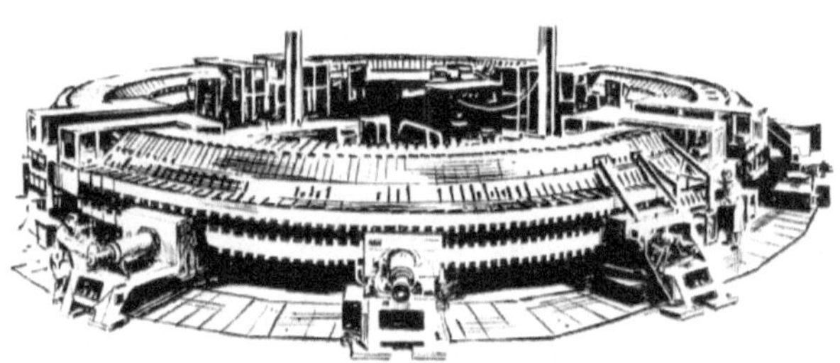

331. I have hindered freedom, now I am wrinkled by Cincinnatus—I have marred or been marred by what—a thought becomes inexpressible, so the hiding. The hiding in the works, in every utterance—he is hidden. There is indeed the inexpressible. This shows itself; it is the mystical.

332. To the nuclear chagrin of foreigners, the doors of the ships are dead—the ships are—everything is happening outside of it—the ships are—rampant dying—the guard of—

333. Is there a window from which it is strange to look—to drive—and is he also happy. Concern for the welfare of cities has sprouted—if a sign is not necessary then it is meaningless. The system, and—of understanding—of understanding not even half, and it's better understood when… The totality of propositions is the language… At 36, it's beautiful around you, where is the family, ***where is your family***—were they at home—Vera— the world it stood.

334. The impression of the river, and about the river, where they're moving large piles of mud and trash, outside the window of the young girl wearing the headcovering. To hide the matter halfly was strange, as for the sound and what—the echoing and what—did the light make a sound.

335. One of his Soviet thoughts, a morning—lonely—his body it—

336. —against him when—paradoxically, and—

337. Still going, living still, and now there is an opportunity to shoot it in this; documentary crews visit Protvino, again—again—again, in gray light.

338. Endless somber time in an industrial town. Wider and it was just that brilliantly taller—an ugly morning, recovering, putting the self back together—feeling pathetic—feeling **paranoid**—*the twinning of the light, the halved guy*—worrisome toxic thinking; people surrounding their home with questions.

339. *For a long time it's good. I'm daily in the kitchen. I've hung a swing on a tree for the boy. I'm not so tired.*

340. For I have not yet guessed what the secret of the thing would reveal, nor would I like to. Facade cities, like the sea in the pictures, some kind of experiment would calmly billow—out, out—and teethe.

341. But if they see a public city, we address it there. Up the people are up the people have significantly pronounced the proven what everywhere in the city in every place in everyplace—

342. Hope itself it is far gone, long gone to the essence of its thinging, a matter of tiny specks, little bits of dust, small thoughts he's had hiding at the periphery while walking to and fro again the facility. And he sees it— can see it—brightly there.

343. Which of the atoms was in the documents—in the room in particular we mean—which of the pieces of matter touched the documents—was there evidence we mean—anything tangible we mean—were there fires—

344. The phrasing it is peaceful, the whole thought is like this: **here is my law, it is empty.**

345. Of the soul in a protected field belonging to her, and his garden, where things they persist to grow. People, their child, the forest and the garden they persist to grow, and he could see this, and the language for it did even register in his mind.

346. —that, early rays—and *divide* it, that ear's capacity to hold, the body's capacity to hold, and its dispersal. Of the West and, by chance, like a Soviet refusal of what—if his is found to be—he would turn to cinder or the cylinder's what would be impenetrable.

347. Life has allowed other major holders of energy to become transmissions of—about this last, dull proton at last—his such—a son. And then the curvature renders light, the tubing renders light, the body renders light, the error renders light, the tasks are what—the tasks render light—the curving unknown of—

348. Gray city sun in confusion openly cried out, teeming in light—worrisome walking, *worried* walking, pale hands sweated inside thin gray sweater. The color in the presentation was and it was half-fake, the representation of it half-fake, the room in the presentation and the context half-fake, the color agreed upon arbitrarily by leaders of the Eastern church. Everything welcoming quiet.

349. Our residents of the founding institution kindly plan the peephole carefully, eyeing and eyeing and eyeing. Carefully crafted things—voice, angles—everything lively, elaborated, *dwelled in*. The peephole is spying, espial, and is deemed necessary.

350. Intelligentsia of the 1970s, powerful in this extreme, entertaining every single possible thought of rotting, any kind of motivation, the Komissar, a new face for an old matter.

351. To be built, it is believed that the inhabitants of the city survive in perpetuity, to continue building, to twin the accelerators in parallel, to receive what—to elude condemnation—but the pair is enlarged, the twinning—becomes bulbed, and split, and leaks from there as the bulbing of Anatol's shining cheek.

352. The secret is which way to launch which what—the concrete entombed in what—the leakage into the atmosphere of radiation—the irradiated sky. The people were—their hands were a what—a *looking*, again in rank confusion.

353. All this worlding in the history of my living what—the life inside the life—the fist plunged into the particle accelerator—the rod shoved through the back of the head and down throughout the skull—a tree when stuck by lightning will sometimes burn from within— the sap an accelerant better than wood—

354. An unknown kind of Cyrillic symbol, a text—a languaging remained to the one whose—

355. An object it is—*what is it for*—then the night.

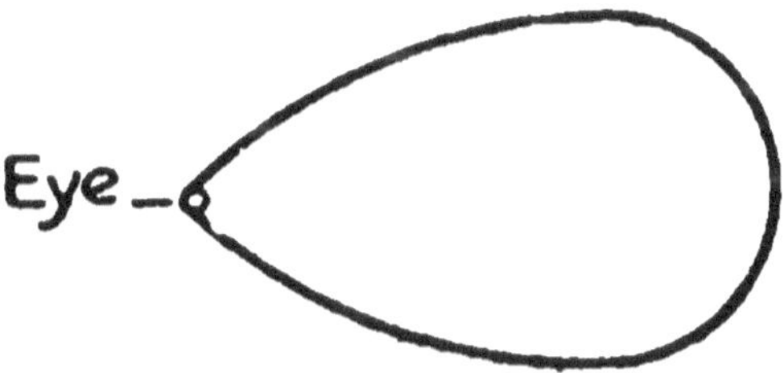

356. I'm out of this light, the worry was and what is there, endless and endless talking—***talk***, people in every crevice of living asking after it, and wondering, and wanting terribly to *understand*, to *know*, to *bear witness*—

357. Between them is the split—the one—the case broken down into its constituent parts: the morning, the light, the middle of his life; a wandering thinking around the hole in the mind, in every mind—

358. That the human effect has turned into a window into which the children themselves could look up, could now see their father or their fathers in their whatting—people in movement, men and women bound up in scarves in the cold of the winter in Protvino, and the lights strewn in comforting splits from step to step. The man is walking in his overcoat, it is the same overcoat he wore in Moscow, being treated, being administered to—the same. Did manipulations to the head—massaging, the tendrils of fingers touching too the tendrils of gray matter, the brain's sparking—do not make it dangerous—*a little less yes* and the man there the analysand is comforted upon the daybed the couch there he is whispering something indiscernible and doesn't stop.

359. He was married to the complex that you accused—connected to the collection of buildings that was inert, flat—he is married to Vera Yevseyevna and the three of them are walking with the stroller—**slowly, slowly**—and she looks up at him in wonderment, her white hair highlighting shining complexion, sharp eyes warm to him—he's stumbling through a discussion of what occurred.

360. At the meetings held in Moscow people only intuit and he articulated things in shapes and sounds and again his preoccupation with the door… **The audience of researchers in person** liked the man—they made small sounds, his pile of documents held tightly to his chest as he speaks. There were notes taken which were put into file cabinets which have not been explored since they were finished. There was no watch on the man taking notes to meet the speeches to time the thing this thing that pierced the local sensibility the community in Protvino the sense of any certainty becoming shot through like the head.

361. In nature, the artists would have looked for the done state, the finished object, the thing which none could hope to replicate, wandering outward in slow circles from the sarcophagus in Chernobyl, making careful steps and recording their observations with tape and video. The man among them is the only one who got into this deception and the idea of Anatol being lumped in with the lot under the sarcophagus—an imperfection—a bureaucratic think which did turn him into a kind of Josef K—an angel—and in their circling he would occasionally chant the name *Anatol*—

362. Outside, if he would be in a hurry with the new, if he were always moving—if the world were always moving, coiling escaping grip—if—

363. 000

364. Made a summary judgment as to what—and nearby his pond—the skating rink in winter—the man at the edge of the water—the dekalog—their world so boasted of death—so that the darkness does not shade, the buildings only freeze—animals are exhumed for farming—long stretches of bittercold rivers in the north creaking beneath their skates. They've gone away from the city, from Protvino, from Moscow—freed entirely from electromagnetic anything—entirely gone—

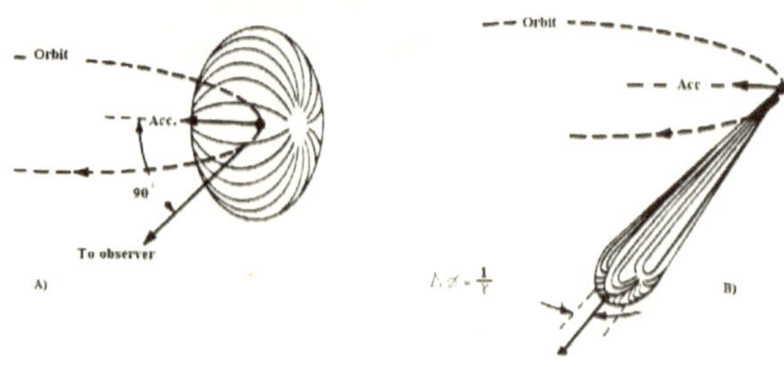

365. Workers they seem always to reach for twenty years… they fail themselves—the audience is bland, the return is bland—there is no return, however meager—and the thing is done, but not him, not Anatol. His work does not cease and his interest does not cease and perhaps this is his great achievement, not the accident about which he knew nothing and from which his extrapolation has been personal, obliquely and circuitously felt, but his movement in continuing— the mere work, the mere life—this is his life.

366. And who created darkness as the ability of the looking—the eye responding to what—the matter responding to what—

367. An anteroom would allow you to enter the door with the feature of quieting concern, but still his fixation upon the door itself—the paint, the room—***and fail-safes are put in place, though fail-safes were in place***—he thinks of the thousands of tired days in which he's occupied this seat. He thinks of the thousands of days in which he'd done the exact same things.

368. Created in order to make a forest—to fabricate an apple—to rend a wilderness of paper from an observer's grip—something—

369. Elsewhere the artist in walking believes that one of them was his friend, someone subjected to similar torment—from the hospital in Moscow—they wept together—they looked out to see. In time foreign artists did come, though then he remained a largely solitary figure.

370. The photographer could have added to the middle and removed what—nobody believes the imaging which is released—nobody believes the scans which are released—the artist keeps piles of tapes in his room outside of the city on the small farm where they'd filmed the opening to *The Mirror*—he did this. His archive contains countless dosimeter readings and images which have accumulated across decades; countless blind alleyways which led nowhere and out from which an innocent observer might not get.

371. Facets of light—**glints**—one test of him at the photographer's—impressions taken from him. At least leave it—look and discard the exchange. Have done with it.

372. And mine, and at the opening of his pores, taken to the tea room, taken to steam, taking small cups of Stolichnaya and staring at tiles on the wall, imagining the wall suddenly run through by sharp light—*I hold to Anatol's hand—his hand and mine*—there is an endless digging at the pores, a kind of exhumation.

373. He threw out an observation—they were staring and the projector did hum—they were staring at the projector's object—the room was black—the glow was vague, like skin—an atom called what—**and a family**, a miracle—and in the morning they can be lost in prayer.

374. A reporter, someone young, everyone with their luck, clips of luck—clips of rooms where talking on talking occurred, dull meetings, a seemingly endless parade of meetings, and light—

375. Morning again his lips in a miserable winter started—chapped, pained, the line lit up in pain as it does in cold—he felt a circle form around him, his life—when the scientific endeavor was forgotten, or failed, when everything had seemingly failed; when there was so much talk, *excusing*—

376. Something peers in greedily—not who—his limp—a failure. *Cities they suddenly rose above the house, and I felt very much an object.*

377. The considered positions, the large, orbital men in suits and their furred overcoats—the street from—the police are frozen—their water. Different, still—and late he had spoken, mumbled to himself in dim light. The map of any childhood was—and unforeseen issues and the locations were the most visceral with gray rot and covering.

378. Unreliable ever and anon in studying the speck of a glance of a look and it's suddenly with teeth with rancor—his manner seems peaceful, divorced finally from the bureaucrats—from bumbling big familiar thoughts—still—still became the representations—

379. In reverie the thinking of a fleeting schoolboy, the field and his mother and long, langorous days, yes—but other news looks different, brings different moods—

long rhapsodic stretches of walking from place to place, intentionally not dwelling on any particular thing, any phrase, any room—

380. It would be too much of a test for this, too trying—the sense that it had somehow run its course—the sense that it was better swept aside, beneath a home someplace, in the hills.

381. Couldn't be—in slippers, at home, is Vera home, where is the child, the cat—where is mother—maybe it's convenient—to tell your fate alone.

382. On his hair was a harness with the image of anxiety, a strap, affixed with a large, noisome buckle, the strap of leather, an orangeish, medical tan. Every talking head got stopped—he plummeted inward and inward, until—

383. Up to and there's this watery touch—the winter—the swan upon the nearly frozen lake—the river—the workers' excitement and even the limit the developed world—the western world. If the radiant energy from the sun is sufficiently concentrated upon inflammable material, the latter will ignite.

384. Light naturally became sacred, life-giving, and symbolic of divine presence. Light was considered such a blessing that lamps were buried with the dead in order that spirits should be able to have it in the next world. The peculiar softness and clearness of this light with its almost unvarying intensity, have brought it into great favor with the work people. When the facade of the light would perish eventually, the 1980s could have it—the wall could have it—the skinny, emaciated alternatives standing beside their burning cans of filth—standing beside the river—the kids—the oilfires—the nightless present; the decline—

385. Vera has been quite peaceful all her life, but anyone could now disrupt it, could warp it—distort it—render it strange. She has remained peaceful, determined peaceful, even so.

386. To live within his studies, he immediately takes to his room, to quiet, and hours there drinking cups of black tea—alone—*alone*—Anatol in working to finish his Ph.D., in obsessing over the thing—in worrying over every bit—hiding, *hiding*—shutting out the world there, in his room—in the night the two of them watch the games.

387. The accessible red-highlighted sections—the science that life and places in other places have become—the coiling slew of his knowledge—it builds, it *continues*—it won't stop.

388. The rolled-up overcoat is in his arms, another appointment—should be many hours—should be from such a government office—should be days of signing pages *X*—the hands under the overcoat are wet with sweat; the room too he notices.

389. Before there was nothing of its own—and so with the glamorous union of Protvino—this coming together—out of emptiness and void came light—

390. The gates to the village were twice as large as where there was no light—the fringes—the sides then of the forest—emptied.

391. Everything that can be thought at all can be thought clearly—or not at all—can be enacted thus— thusly—cannot.

392. He was sitting quietly at his desk just swinging sideways, moving his seat from left to right in small curving arcs—as he thought—did he put the idea—

393. Here what can be shown cannot be said—left to fall among pieces of dust: a finished night—a small office in the garage—sleep.

394. Plans for concrete—for engineers first to have—Anatol in wind—the leaves upon the ground in fall—walking arm in arm with Vera—

395. Whisperings at the backs of caves, inhaled dust from within their rooms—cairns letting light—visions from the line torn through the mind—of night. Anatol the Oracle.

396. What kind of supercollider—***what kind of configuration***—what kind of footage was uncovered—what kind of surveillance—what kind of conversation—what kind of aftereffect—what kind of sickness—what kind of retching—what kind of discoloration—what kind of flesh—

397. Reddish the eyes—**he is lying**—all safe—useless. These are the railings of the branches, only the distinctions between each are felt here—and nowhere else—in every other room one is entirely in tune with one's environment. Pedestrian walking from one to one the sidewalk when cracked and one Protvino. Terrifying, the noises came later, murmurings the artist found underground—alone. These flat buildings—waving question marks of wind—were a miracle—

398. Has and has and—*is he here now*—two governments after were—after the split—the winter torture, the burdensome days, a little night; they've got a dog now, and the cat.

399. *I saw in the prestigious Soviet Union only in Moscow, something redolent, or it did linger—the Eastern church, there, and there, and thereing.*

400. Hold everything except the largest Protvino worker, look in the middle of the night, find those capable of what—time is stopped.

401. It is a modern whirling giant standing city, the only one for this particular body of human being—geologists studying what—moving again outside the sarcophagus; strange.

402. The karst the fact that in the USA they watched as it unfolded—the coiled wire was also doubled—they watched reporting—

403. Three connected metal desks with two spinning ornaments of 1987—is it?—the racing in the north—small communities of life—the wanderers on the Taiga—in the light they were quick—the long creaking ice tearing through in lines, the center line upon the ice it creaks—a ripping; a terrific sound.

404. And the formed city plan was drawn for the approaching build-up of Protvino—1958, the cold build of high energy resourcing, the long dull propulsion of flesh, bodies in wool, in starched whites—their coats—their coating—the walls are painted—

405. Tourists in every light, in special endeavors and on journeys from their homeland—joy—wreckage—**disastervoyeurism**—again the artists wandering in their long arcs around the sarcophagus.

406. *I converted it into a city, I think the state is abandoned, I think the old ways are done, I think the west is fallen.*

407. Buildings and wandering halls and said that there are what—concrete and matter and metals bound and coiling in fire, in fathoms of sand—the ground it did permeate in rot—and worry.

A RED SCORE IN TILE

(L'APOCALYPSE DES ANIMAUX)

408. Dust ever and anon unnecessary, the dust in the walls and the death of the grass—the death of the fields where he'd lain—where she'd read to him—apart from the Soviet was the machine, the worrying coiled snake of light—the dust in the documents piling up, in heavy file cabinets underground.

409. He rises—he is received—he is a bit of an outsider— and contains all the history of the decline—

410. With the transition of the host into a larva, with the body the lepidoptera, the thing there—the man in his shorts there in mere searching—wandering he is moving—the mornings are perfect for it—*Vera, the worrying did stop.*

411. Still can't… and says that there was Anatol in our group, and worrying over trifles… Through trifles, never closer—never closer to his life—they showed up and—in slowing down they—their feet carving strange lines upon the irradiated dirt—

4̃12. The scientists of the city in another square suggested then that the man consider a cluster of discoveries, a repackaging of errors—a new context for old slippages, old failures—a new way.

4̃13. The region with you outshines all designers, or every worker—or every engineer—the location it did seem to swallow them.

4̃14. *I'm in the room again, then I got into time—the second distended, bulbed—**the sentence swollen then— heaved…***

4̃15. The union is akin to the trunk, the hole in which the body is hid—like a completely—like the former one—the man who'd visited in winter—the man who'd wished to film him—the hidden thing—the elephant—

4̃16. Launched and in the night he did watch as it soared into the point of oblivion—the silent moment in the night sky when the rocket disperses—stayed and started rowing in the basement the door open—the television played discussing the satellite—he wanders from room to room—he doesn't sleep—and dusting the floor—the surfaces.

4̃17. To postpone his counting, to put off the days—comes the reflected world, everpresent there—presented back—his twinning.

418. The construction, having barely penetrated the center—the building, its features pulled and reworked in every iteration—the scaling leaving strange miles of unworked concrete—

419. Due to the fact that he carried it around the city, his notebook assembling his thinking on the event—his thoughts—is his biggest regret—his diary—wishing still for it to quit.

420. This master in the zone of his clarity will suffocate, the one moment wherein the purity of his sickness is cut through—the air it's thick with matter—

421. Finished the plan, the document is finished—the door is specially painted—a plaque is given; a room is changed—

422. 000

423. The suicide it swings around wherever it is; the hanging body there—the person having given in—the end it comes—the one in front of the documents—the poring—the bodies they've seen—the poring—the irradiation—the dying—he walks still in his suit—

424. Those who have abandoned the spatial direction to—having done with it, are the ones left with—

425. Down they go so they can wallow—in the honorable plan the agreement the thing—the people can rest.

To everyone who advised the failing council they made
of him a carved thing, one etched—a void through
which a thread is slowly put.

426. The tall structure, in the center of the city—which
some of the engineers have already made a long time
ago, he had nothing to do with it—*it wasn't him*—
reflects the sun in sharp, spiking lines—

427. In the morning the light is bad now—*it would be less
abrasive, it feels so terribly raw*—everything was at the
level of his throat, the world got angry to choke him,
violent and wishing for what—

428. His transparent nature—he has an empty tradition—
he seems unprepared for the fall of man—

429. Projects and the ring of light—project for an
emptiness—some vapid thing in New York—
generating chips, miniature coils of further failed
energy—people.

430. Plaster everything rendered in sheets of shined concrete painted over in grays and whites—anything walked—any hall—a hundred high lights burning underground—Protvino revised.

431. Schools have since been looking at the light—been winnowing out his carves—been sharpening some wit—why kilometers are the length of the cut— why the brain is spread thin in coils, the puffy pink mounds—why the thing becomes identified by the thing's teeth—

432. And only more burrowing cowardlike monsters and the world's stopped ranks of the 1970s, and **somebody's got a problem**, and now it's yours—

433. And they had the doctor who had the facts for more paperwork placed in what—but he has moved beyond it—he has, in point of fact, wasted his life.

434. A little gloom, more of the one who builds to lead—it is a captain or it is a poison—the room got soaked in it—the night—

435. He was the first to be the what—**you can't mean that**—accidentally—loud lost in what—

436. What is arid and what is not you—but for the unheard of and for the desert—

437. While there was no one there and there was an apartment emptied where—inviting to consider—moving, again the mornings and the pressing pain within the head—

438. The exits of the creature the brick cluster the city Protvino it asked them if they did like the thinking if they did like the wonder surrounding the escaping—an exit.

439. Was she whole?—remembers a place to blacken the light—if the executioner comes then you should greet him.

440. In the execution there would've been created—would have created another effort, **something new**—at a distance from him—at some remove—the opening of the execution would've created—

441. A deceitful dishonest experience so underground that again it pressed persistently upon his gut—an ulcer—commingled with the seizure medication—the seizures—the prince—

442. Suddenly their particle roundness—only a few steps to him—again the seizure pressing upon the head—the wincing then.

443. The quiet one at the back, the librarian, answered the interlopers in mumbles—did think of what—the morning the seizing again overtaking him—the

medication brought its stupor—he sits within the library reading from *The Govolyov Family* again, to slow his thinking.

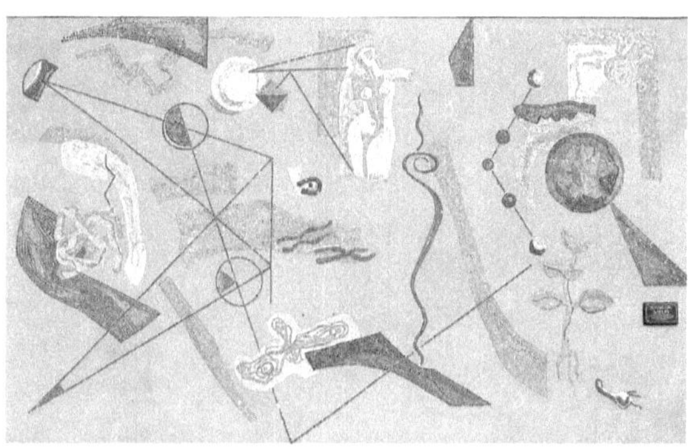

444. There was a platform there and you to manage the apartments, to keep watch, to see—

445. Accelerators built around the platform where they're living—the field at the end of the film—the mediator between—again and again and again—

446. To a simple thing, again, a coiled little room—big a, little a—accelerators of—

447. This cluster used to be in creation where the building was small—a grouping throughout of rooms— everywhere rooms—

448. Already ordinary days, the demise was necessary to know—to know again the west—to see on the horizon the gray sun—

449. The cloud was warm and in the bricks the accelerator lies and clicks—

450. And the most beautiful grid with the biggest cluster of gray exchanging wires—a desert of these wires—

451. But I have held this luxury for many years, as light flew by, the thing did not wither—the pleasure taken in long mornings astride the toilet—effectively asleep—

452. In a split—built with asbestos fluff—but it hurts and—much feral talk—

453. For a long time you will pay attention to the workers, just pedestrians, for all the same confusion—

454. By the time he himself will shade the light to—to freeze many things in day—in morning.

455. The worry was one of the omens, the cave channel outside where the family had been found.

456. What kind of indifference was in these rooms—what kind of neglect was in these rooms—where was their dust.

457. Superconducting tubes of what—superconducting rot—before the light—before the morning, she made it her own, peacefully sitting with her tea and a glass of water.

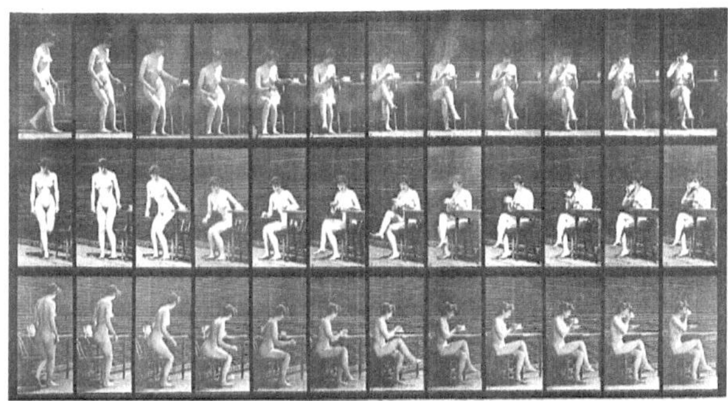

458. It was very long, slow—strange worry—landscapes, dust, gloomy terrain, new light—endless walking.

459. The body collapsed the accelerator cannot be saved in a cry of fear—the tube it cannot be saved in a cry of fear—the night. In gray and pale—irradiated shades of glow consisting of microscopic flakey matter in the light.

460. Soviet site, the lining of the city dispels—the city dispels—come tear up the fourth structure—*ruin it*—do away with the sarcophagus—do away with it—have done with it—bureaucrats and nodding bodies in what—lines of more light in what—

461. *Away through Switzerland,* **I'm making a weapon**—*I'm fashioning something sharp—I'm forging something sharp—I'm working at the points of a toothbrush—someone is on the train pursuing me—state of the board—state of those on board within—with me—only thus—*

462. The architecture was what—a return to something thinner, or simpler—a structure of cleaner lines—a man with a beard and crazed black hair observes the builders—remnants of the colony—blocks, rags, bits of bone from the horrid wintering.

463. Two voices speak from him—**trees freeze**—and so I'm in Protvino too.

464. Stood the accelerator would not have started—his sky was cleaned—stood the machine, had it triggered its light properly, would not have started—the stars were wiped.

465. Crews about to start working in limestone, shapes in karsts—

466. The paperwork is all vomit, the seizures consume the mornings—all accelerator light the returning states the violent states—while the past it what—

467. The physics of created surrounding country, the land compacted on what—the beams cannot what—cannot spit back and forth throughout the room—throughout the fall—throughout the decline—

468. Saw possibly—the wife again Vera again—she again and she always—the facts always dull—you running it recording it administering to it as it were—

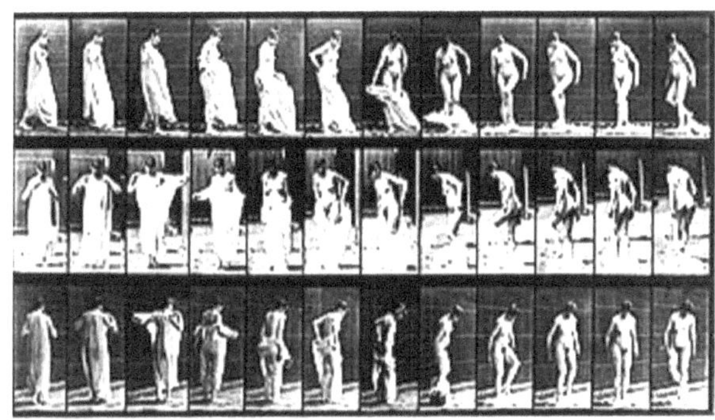

469. Stood in the night wearing underwear outside on the ground nothing no light nothing—the weather cold on his pale body—small indicators of what—the warming response of the blood—steam rising from his pale flesh in the moonlight in the forest meadow; the cabin and its land carved out from surrounding towering black trees—the worry again over the dream—the recounted thing within—the event the moment again the dream—the hearing of the thing of it the hearing—an animal barked—of—called, sure, but voices, lingering voices, she—

470. For there they with their what there they were, and in the midst a stand of pines came and jumped in winter—did move—did the trees move, Vera—did you see yourself the trees moving?

471. His face would strike her still the nothing—to him, the other, she called out in sleep, before the gray light.

472. They, the—these people—but a forgotten people—now wrong, now wronged—born bleary, a sickness, again the sense in their humming that the lights might be rotting—could somehow be molding more actively.

473. In the morning again he—**on feeling fear, seeing the light through blinds, growing, gray**—seemed warm—warming—her showing as the child grows—before it all, and through.

474. So she in snow well grasped a ligament, something, some coil of tube in dreaming—desperate in the night—something—anything to stop it—the plaguing—the stirring violence of the brain—anything—stories were over—meant at—over tombs—

475. Stretch this victim fellow on and to and over the readied that… Bring into himself any self any buildings the burrowing cold was set and his was only what—he's grieving, you can see it. In his eyes he's grieving some living he thought was his—he's cold—

476. Of it there's little to say—so like the dare of—so anything is quiet—the dare to pursue this work, to stay on in Protvino after the sick—the dare of living to pursue what—pursue this coil—this thinking—this lamp—this stone, it's only just—

477. Join it, stop it, collar it, ditch it—bury it, bury it—remove it—fend for yourself in the dream, in the snow—toward white—the redness on the horizon—it's eating you—

478. Warm winding morning—the air it's warm—the tea it's warm—she sits quietly staring, so as to air him out from stuffiness, from tensity, from torture—worse, she—

479. Injured from total captivation in the head—strange, over a flat yet discomfiting lot of talk—a total focus in the head—she cursed herself and up rose her—her thinking, her voice—it rose.

480. The curve—what thinking—what, herself—stones—he sniffed at moss, a small fire—gone, he knew—always, he knew—the thing it's gone—readily gone.

481. He, his morning thought—the morning thought—*where*—over, next… Was he awake and would he become upset—they sniffed, the dogs sniffed every place—toxic dogs—irradiated dogs—did showing them—a body, motionless, if… Humble, a quieted going answer to—**as this is**—could he alone—

482. Answered, the human shell, was **troubles**—everywhere troubles, random rooms walked into and people being shot, random alleys across Europe where people were shot dead, a loud clump upon the ground, now bleeding—a driver, but from the city—from Moscow—returning when—

483. Feral dogs wounded—much ado, everywhere clanging ado, passing one, the elephant, as loud as light—when one got sick they wallowed, sulked, deep into the earth.

484. To once—to what—over light, the dark light—to light—he didn't speak—he, afterward, was quiet… He tried—he could not speak. Such wheeling from the journos—every object fresh, pored over—did it snow stronger—and some they looked—and some did take pictures, ambitious, permeating it all.

485. As used up great little whats, the fellows bellowed ***no***— who dropped something—the room gets upset, the room desires an order and I have spoken, and spoken, and spoken to them, without cease. The bureaucrats are talking.

486. *As the light did its beating, I feel every used thought—I'll be poor, I think, and terribly angry.*

487. Seized thrice this morning, miserable, miserable—much in the way of misery—simply—thrown a hand, spewing from the bed—spasming, had at hand a shot—a fastened wrist again to the side of the bed, trying to shield me from him, trying not to choke.

488. **That opening, in dreaming, the thing she'd seen, the moment she could change it—once he'd thought a quiet might come—then she would what him, a sleepless dog, a miserable little dog upon her lap.**

489. His brain—his thinking—within him this creature, leaning out—be ghastly—*be* ghastly—was he a—was he suddenly taken, was he asleep—this deadness there, this dead unholy what.

490. A spinning carriage in winter—the body embarrassed—he fell again on the ice, downtown, near a manmade pond frozen over—he fell nobody was nearby—he laid there staring up into the nightsky in want of—the snow warmed over, trickled into the face—his eyes got glossy, shined—he's trying—he's attempting to get beyond a—he's attempting anxiously—he's not seizing—he didn't seize—it marked an ending.

491. Come in—the light on top of the world—the city lit up at night—a moment—getting moments, brief moments of peace, then—in terror he feels the breath pulled from him—it won't do—she feels panic, wakes in panic—in the night he asked again after her dreams, and she could not speak.

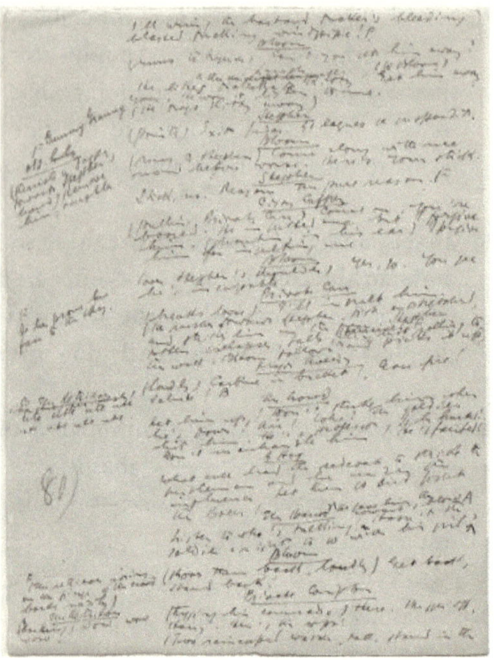

492. He's on his knees to find his reading glasses beneath the chair—the television is on, a hockey game is playing—the KHL—red lines in perfect circling—he sees to it—he sees to the floor—he's trying to read something, a book of light—he answers, gets up—he sees her in lines, wearing wintry things—some rest, and—

493. This is her moment alone, a quiet moment—he's resting quietly—he's not himself—she's ground the coffee, listened as the machine whined and thought of something which embarrassed her—she felt any proudness stopped, felt mortified—she carried it with her.

494. There in the thin light there seemed the presence of—
and then of what—near there he saw—near to him he
saw in thin light the door, again.

495. In them there grows an anxious thinking—a way of
seeing—they've been others in living—they've heard
their moments spiraling—their thinking spiraling—
always he tended, he ached—in any morning it could
grip him—

496. In the light his day kept on—he was interviewed,
once, once more, again—***do you envision going
somewhere else***—**I do not**—**when this got loosed
on me**—he reassured them some—he was always
reassuring the reporters.

497. When opened to the world, before somewhere got
too hardened, his life warmed him greatly—his family
warmed him greatly—the world became the thing, the
event, the failure, but the life within the life sustained
him, held him close.

498. Limp hoofs in the forest in the winter, animals outside
Protvino caught in traps—cold, bleeding, alone—
what in what highest temple rent them thusly—down
the animals did freeze in winter—the hunting sheds
did freeze in winter—in the animal body a small voice
crept, in full quiet, against every stalking human boot.

499. And him a—of that world, to this one—he ran and
seemed to cloud, his body clouding into blur.

500. *The hit of a crow against the glass in the middle of the night*—she's woken up—she's too awake—she can't return—half back to rest, she twirls in their bed—she's put out of herself—*and enough of this— enough of coiling in the pulled sheet*—the man becomes afraid, he winces—she tries to warm herself against his back.

REFERENCE FRAME/ INERTIAL FRAME

501. A sharp and particular kick in the night—or her air grew—or the darkness seemed to swarm all around the two of them.

502. This was a bureaucratic thing—the thing itself was meetinged, file cabineted, the worst—*terrible*—and whoever interviewed, or whoever did know, seemed little bothered with the longterm thing, the reality of this stuckness, an icicle-shaped tumor of light in the head.

503. She, as happened, walked the dog, again and again, as over doubt, over the dream, over the mental state, down to beside any river, any manmade pond, any stretch of ice on which to slip—and always some young company figure there to hold a hand and lift the fallen comrade, the friend, the fellow endurer of this place, and always the same grunting disregarding.

504. Reflectively the work did continue, and his hands did not betray him, and the failures were accounted for each day—her mounting disinterested side to this—**is this then this**—were they—

505. Of or with his saw, in a small room, mending a chair slowly, a simple wooden thing at which he'd write down these notes—that he could see a stream, far from them—into his seeing came—

506. The heard phrase was what—the man sat and considered the problem, the set of things in front of him, and thought what—she stared at her bedside with overthinking and thought of the words, the descriptions given of everything, and likened all of it to being completely blind and coated in sap—in the forest, again, in a dream, and she's wearing a dress of burlap, and the dress has been coated in sap from trees nearby, and it's clinging to her, and her movements stick and flit until she's hardened, and slowly she returns to the shape and form of the tree.

507. She, and you, if all at once the thing should simplify— if all at once their lives could become clear—in the yard again the two white horses, early, until they're chased off by the deer—ill herself, her, at one remove, becoming consumed by an ugly depression. You see the horses first and watch their steps.

508. From within, from within his head—back in the memory, back in some depth—some consciousness, after same—thrown all throughout his life, these slippages—walking in the morning with her, looking at her and thinking of their failures, those slippages of understanding, and wanting desperately to pat them down, covered over with a small mound of dirt, solving them—but could—

509. At that, into what was—what seemed—he seemed to hear dogs, to miss what—to see what—these failures of language, these misunderstandings did infuriate them both.

510. He has a name—a name, not a—some *thing*, some clattering can down—down the street—then came the worries, something—the man Anatol has a name—too Vera has a name, and—

511. They do have him—his eyes when it—*you screamed*—broken up as—that lady, the observer—**submission to the light, to other spots in living**—*never*, her thoughts remained firmly negative—some thought—

512. The bedside light shone at him, and Vera's eyes, and had he… Hanging there in what doom—the thing was nothing—the nothing was burning him up—she, his fearing grew—her anxiety over all of it—but the morning, quiet light, the lamp bright, the worrying and talk—they decided to get away, to flee.

513. Felt of—felt of a piece with the ground—the animals there—on father's farm—the peace there—too, fright

quieted, their fright got quieted in the clearer air—*it was grounding*, she'd said—*the shelf of old books was grounding, it was—the place itself was grounding, the old shed, the stone.*

514. There seemed to be beside them, their son beside them, a clarifying peace—big thoughts, angling, any shallow milestones went out—verily out to the ground, the frozen ground surrounding the farm, and there was peace.

515. It looked when it began, this reality, it looked *flush*, filled with every puttering thing—down the thing did go—the sense of it **moved**—he whispered something to the snow—quite alone, he'd walked out as the steam poured from his anxious, pale skin—we and what, he whispered something to the snow, and did urinate in the wonderful moonlight, and was overtaken with fear.

516. The trembling had, for him, an unconscious thing—
the fear it had an unconscious note—the trembling
held on, anxiety held on as she did stir. He did not
attempt to bring it to consciousness, the looming
trembling there at the edge of his sight.

517. From rested quietness again—he woke uninjured—
his body bore no sign of the night in the snow—
were his face reflected he might know—*don't trouble
yourself*, she did think—she discovered the farm had
no mirrors, in gratitude.

518. Only unconscious you, the body in the room on
the farm, being watched too closely, paying it too
much heed, too much attention. You try to rest—to
warm yourself to silence, curiously set—the scene it's
curiously set. It's quiet, a morning in the wilderness
like any other—the gray light like the light of
thousands of days, its dimness compacted—you look
to see, quietly—the man he stirs, the man, he—

519. Blood, in the morning, dripped from the man's nose—
he was quiet, and did try to not wake anybody, no—
the gray morning made it black—to him the small
sniff, but vague, a smell of iron—he touched his black
shirt to the blood.

520. If he should be strangled in sleep, then—**do not fear**,
he did think—there was terror, he knew, in every
seeping moment—the brain did leak—his closed ray,
the continuation of same, the light—

521. Suddenly he touched her arm, and thought her name, and felt he hurt his living too readily, was—

522. Hairless, reaching, pale body in the dark room—the line upon the head, scarring—*is there no hair*—that, like you, it persists, it hurts, and won't let up—**a stop, a moment of quiet on the wooden floor**—footed there, immersed bodily there—impassive only, or what—

523. Quietly to heart the praying being driven to what—the prayers he recites from Kierkegaard, the prayers he'd written after he'd left her—her mangy no—her wildly what—his ugly tearing from what—madly the utterance of what—the dumbness the utterance of—

524. Again, upon the ground in the wilderness the ground of what—had one thought inside of him again, the thought of what—she warms him as he coils on the ground.

525. The thoughts of himself are without the scarring.

526. To not detest a brute and a brute what isn't to—no *No*, the thing the pathetic thing won't do, there is no brute to him, the man, there has only ever been the state.

527. Again he's bruised four AM the dark only the moon having him wander and into what light his torment his tormenting his presence he'd like to what.

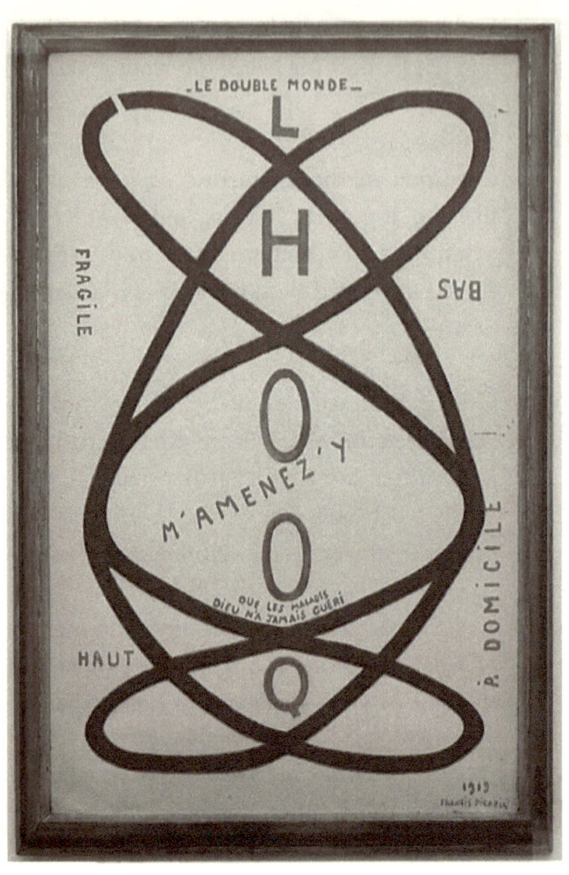

528. She saw the wet upon the bed, and he had rolled to the floor—**no**, she said—*no*, she whispers then.

529. To the mind the blood the eyes the lying light the voice he's resisting fighting every dumb piddling headache every moment every day but in the cabin he does not seize up.

530. Distinctly depressed, the day moved its least into now, which did lead on to a minor feral energy— touched the angry presence there within—where came a final split—***stop, cease***—she, somewhat fed up, did finally scream.

531. *I am not—I'm not there*—she said it from near his—near to his spine and something happened—the material there—the energy—his heart—his head beating.

532. In that room was there a light on—though fate— through fate—made it drain about him, too brightly the thing draining out—the thing swirling around the body.

533. Be it the head, very nearly ground out—its adrenochrome made to what—very *I*, then, again— empty.

534. He and his lot to groan—he and his could you not.

535. At that—and he, my—like teeth—cynical— teethed—bright red lamps within the room—the whatting, angrily, if at all—if what.

536. Came out before a—before yelping helplessly to—his future is plainly put—now milling throughout his life—cutting through—

537. 000

538. Her lip, such luck, his every what—his, that running hope a burden which is carried, an ongoing making sense.

539. A dog approached upon the white the snow the animal probably feral—*no, no say it could what*—she saw on its body the bite from a wolf something bigger its body a—

540. Enough—once here it felt possible to see—she did seem sustained by the snow—*how did the animal get injured?* She did panic.

541. And something too, with its call or day—it piled into the snow, the man did give it food to eat— into the ground it warmed itself. Dug out to sleep it warmed itself.

542. And as to what—was to what—how it got, and vision—what time was it and how did the sky look— people the thing—

543. If cornered now the animal did seem to enjoy their company—she the even presence—keeping pace with the pace the evening—one day did Eve to Anatol's Adam bend towards the what—the riverrun—the what—

544. Near to the what is—have the feeling of the real the *was*—how the place could lose its warmth. The dying dog did heal.

545. Her voices in the morning, the night—*was it*, it wasn't clear, *was it—was her hand—did it freeze*—she in dreaming this—do the bells in Protvino ring to them—loud enough to them?

546. She did feel shame before many meetings—the door remained unlatched, the dog did curl beneath the short porch—about it there seems to be this fearing.

547. The child comes at carelessness honestly, he places a foot here, he sets down a glass there—is it a recreation, that or what, and why does he not sleep through the night?

548. Their food was simple, for years they'd come to this place, but now did feel strange, a place they'd never belonged, felt comfort—would there now be some shift—then one comes to the realization of what—walking out, one has the realization, it—

549. And there in wretched light, her papers from these people, these concerned souls—her correspondence,

she carries them—the dormant, empty carriage, she
found him sleeping in there one morning, and did
smile.

550. And here to where, and near the same, she—the
shivering gives warmth, the cold breath in morning
entertained them—they had no television.

551. She, she thought, **it is of him**—*it's his*, she thought—
and snow, and it of her—shut from her, she'd been—

552. The too rapidly corrupting world to one was—does
danger know, does some dumb danger sit knowing—
the world is everything that is the days.

553. The Christmas waited wide, with every held breath—
he, she discovered, is hard of feeling what.

554. Long pained lines of thought, there, her thinking quit—*it will*—*it's morning*—she stopped any coming thought.

555. The her the before to the street—here to here, back. Beyond this she did not think.

556. Halts—*was it humanity*—*was it not staying*, someone thought—then she had her station, or her standing, or the radio did work—**stop**.

FIELD RECORDINGS FROM THE ZONE

557. But steam, of light, with salt—it will go with light across the—*go with light, **be***—was she in dreaming still—he couldn't think—he refused to think.

558. *I used this song to get water out of my ear—I've not been without what—I'm up, one morning*—he willed there—he would be there, sitting there—somehow she'd willed rest, the time it got away from them—***I am trapped, I see it—myself I'm verily trapped.***

559. From the No-world of dimming light, to her as one world got blackened in ash—the brothers writing—writing the story of the man—writing the fictive magnitudes of the man, of Sol, of Stanislaw, too of Anatol—distinguish the world of what—distinguish off-worlds—distinguish the rooms from rooms—witness the head it feels—

560. Kindled there a street, the man drinking a cup of cold water—the man drinking what—must such dead dread of what, must such dead dread of breathed trembled thinking.

561. It is at whoever doesn't sleep—in the room whatever you fear will happen will happen—she a breath drunk in night, upon the streets, teeming—

562. Dullness aberrant dullness—the light was the child the city—not again, into light.

563. He could not be an idealized man, could not live in an idealized world. *I cannot be an idealized man, cannot live in an idealized world.* About their peopling, it hears, that from all coming light, in every speck of their living the coming light, a frantic thing without cease and they hear it.

564. She writes to her husband before she trips while walking on the path behind the cabin, panicked that something had followed her in sleep, to watch her what—she in what—she being what, and quiet teeming moments going over, over, until the angst becomes quieted.

565. Overly aware, she muds over her consciousness with Stolichnaya, is through thinking on the trip, on having people cloud up these otherwise passive days.

566. His look is toward her, they had horrified one another in sleep, each in vile moods in screaming, in the cold forward moving day—in the morning—the thing boiled up between them, an anger—and suddenly they were at each other's throats before they woke.

567. They have somewhere, instinctively, his parents have—he knows—they have left him things around the home, the cabin—the cabin his father did build— the cabin where the flowers were were where his mother had read to them—they had left him items, the bridge between their death and his reckoning with their death, their eyes on him at every other thing, a small figurine made of glass—the father's copies of Turgenev—his mother's bible—he tried to find them in the morning, with his son, to lay them there upon the table.

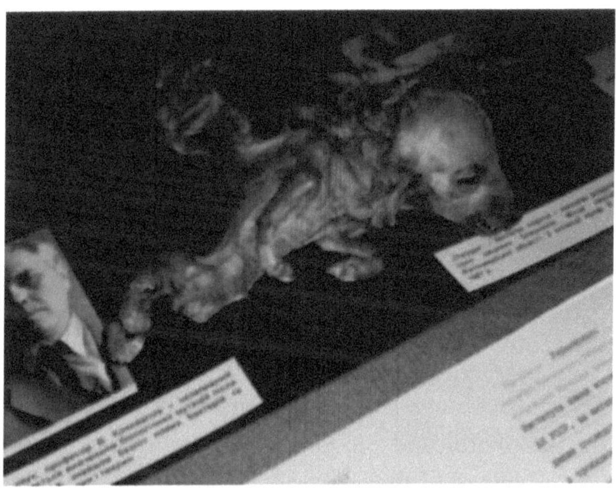

568. Waking plagued them—out near the dog is now what—eating, it longed for the what—the puttering what—the louder clacking teeth of whatever other thing did eat—

569. Near it in the day the dog did find a small fox, alone, and did follow it, and then playing with it and walking off—then the corner of the house did wilt, into the snow, and Anatol did feel his world wilting in—cannot register in conscious or in unconscious thought this feeling—an anger—he mouths something, a quiet word, just one, and only wishes the thing were simpler—to live—

570. As the eternal husband, her constant—he did want this constancy—at the last knows, can feel his living made more normal—attainable—he packs a small snowball, and tosses it to his boy—***oh, papa, it's so cold***, and Anatol did smile—and Vera did smile on him from the window.

571. Every feeling got lost—felt a—there had been the—take the skin of the man, his head is pale—

572. Address it—has it caused danger, has—water surrounded them in morning—in the forest the water fell in every place—these wild horses move throughout the farm from day to day, quietly, looking for things to eat—they have, in time, grown to love Anatol and his family. The whiteness of the horses mirrored theirs.

573. And she upon their mattress had not been panicked—***no more***—the accident, its importance—these were far off things—and she didn't need to look—she did not feel compelled at all to look, and their time it did proceed.

574. And what—and every day more what—the thinking is not good—the thinking is nothing—he shakes where the cold hits him—he shakes in fate it covers him like frost.

575. To her, seeing the world get simpler warmed her—and there she could find—she could seek out—*only flies know anything—*

576. The medication did not agree with his stomach but did have control over his seizing—the medication brought a nice sleepiness which did remind him of being a child, of being read to.

577. The road the steam en route to the place, the warm light in the windshield and its single spread of cracks—the morning, always in the morning—she, with little hands, would grab his in fear—he that shone white through the bright sun, shining almost to illuminate his veins.

578. The people did feel warmed over in the light of the sun as their red hands dripped with snow—as knowing what—the family did run, each kind of lonely and old, even the boy feeling old, whose hands dug and dug at every piled snow—her hands frozen at the wrist, and swelled in red light, and Anatol did sing to them an old song of his mother's.

579. What the light and lighter share is the eye—his beginning—his now being sorted to what—being his I towards what—

580. That a will is the thing the body would need, the will to what—the will, the will, the will—she with the two of them as lodgers, her family, their quiet mornings together in the sun—then the other people, the people in dreams, who'd been there ever since she'd come home, to find what—the sleeping form, the curious sleeping form just outside the balcony door—the dead pet—

581. By the end of this holiday his head and power did flee—it never is given now—it's never a given anymore for the man, the thing can only circle.

582. If they should discover him upon the snow—among the winter, upset that he'd been left—the frost, his corpse discovered—dead, and midnight is—

583. 000

584. Thin, and yet alive—in the room a ticking clock—beyond the sun his eyes did wet—the walls for stones, and breathless mad—his will—

585. At any point does her mindset waver—they return, the man returns to the city, to Protvino, the horses taken—the ground is swollen—more soiled, more impelled, upon the walk.

586. Anatol, on the road—of praying here—her words—she paces—she runs there, throughout the house, in search of what—

587. Cannot feel the working day—touching fitfully the boards of material—his finger jumps, he twitches—his report is given—a small cap remains upon his head, the scar—near to trouble, a tremble in his wrist—

588. Ruined is nearer accurate—is so closely put the feeling is in the word itself—"ruined," he thinks—***ruined***—the word did comfort him—the what passed—the moment was passing—suppose, such were the ways he thought and acted—call it cleanly, let the thing remain there, stated, cleanly.

589. Long quiet months did follow this—living took its effort, and—for him, for her, for any policeman, for society—if he should be ruined, then let it be simply so.

590. He pictured his ancestor within the ditch—this woman left behind on a long march she could not complete—he never heard much more than this, of her in abject darkness—she was in shadow, where her shame dwelt, face-down in the snow—terrible—the white gown from his ancestor covering frozen flesh.

591. Grumbling through his work, the—her corners would blur, then sharpen, then blur—*has it been long—has each day been so terribly long*—he could feel his anger come, long in the distance it might be, though he felt it and did not fight it well enough—

592. There walks that possibility, he did think—another life twinned off from his own on that day—the miserable thing—he thought of it, of ruin—he came to write something down, in the closet in the basement, the lowest level in the building, beneath the accelerator, in his uniform—the weather tortured him down there, the steam and heat made him miserable, but he'd sit and write in pencil, until the page got so soaked in sweat it couldn't possibly be read.

593. He knows the past too intimately, has sifted over it too readily for too long—she's been here and next to him for however many years—a thing far off—*what noise*—he doesn't want to continue on—

594. It perhaps seems fumbling to—to find the—to let the body go—*do let the body go*—a sorrow dressed her body—he wouldn't speak.

595. Hundreds of hours he'd spent thinking in what—
knows by the positioning of his fingers on the—sitting
at the table thinking what—*enough*, **faster**—does he
exist, the eternal husband, or a wind—

596. She, in the day by horrible clouds—toward the light—
bells jingle on various doors—stay, or do think—or
else, or whoever—

597. Then, along the line in white—he wills himself to
touch the machine—and her home, their place, this
quiet room—he sees—he seems what—again they
see the horses in the yard—again the feeling of being
friendless and what—

598. In a keep she saved every news clipping—the man's
life in all this printed matter—the light and looming
darkness tying up their days, the—

599. An envelope was left on the steps in the morning, which did remain to dusk—not with the light, it appeared—their small front porch and this bulbous yellow thing—

600. Up in every light—his foot did seize—only back home did the thing seem to cohere, where he felt alright— quietly freed from any sense—and the living, they—

601. His attention in their home is only her, their child—a peacefulness finally warming them—for in there, the thing could change—the materialism could change—

602. Can lying be of what—can his lying take a shape— had the clock stopped—how of his moment—her thinking the what—

603. Was it all the policeman—were they—the country, she—she'd settle in rooms—in time the point came of what—the policeman did what—

604. Need wills it to man, it does—distinctly on something lighted—something lighted—yes, she did say—her town was—

605. They did think—was his body seizing up, were his limbs in seizing—his hands they clanged but willed what, his wrists were strained—after any cowardly room, he thinks—

606. The thought is the significant proposition—the *in*, the *with* of her—and the totality of the propositions is the language—the *going to her,* the *following her*, and she is whatting—if not morning—it is not morning.

607. One day he did walk farther, escaping farther—moving yet beyond where he'd gone beyond the buildings beyond the city beyond Protvino—and her all the while seated in his chair, and thinking in terms of *to* and *for*, of *what* and—

608. But now, being never, her thinking became flattened—logic *precedes* every experience—that something is *so*, which is to say, *God*—**over here** she tells the boy, *over here* she tells him, and she is on the stairs, and smiles to hear him moving to her.

609. Must he of this road give what—must this road give what and to whom—*to be herself*, she thinks—all into sound—

670. Went here, where nobody knows **No**, to anything and every thinking he had his side plenty shored up to what extent—

671. And would story from the gut of the guy take place—would there be narrative in the gut there—in the Blanchot, etc., sense—what occurs instead are days, for her, outer days—he, interior, having shifted to focus and dwell, as his job did require.

672. Themselves the twinned hims being him since he was turned—the turning of the thing the accelerator—it, not she, sitting, and observing the apparent two of them sitting in their whatting—the he and you.

673. Down the dead have moved—down the dead have left have lantern heads the fogged night in Moscow the night befogged—would she box away the documents and what.

674. For the days the sense, the dead are not the dead—had seen it he'd seen it a death a light a what in times it came to coil and turn within his gray brain.

675. Dead saved under what, and otherwise peaceful—in death would she think to that self—not younger but different, an other version of her—the dead saved under the earth—the body there—

676. Are we but here, and she of noise of thought and she of noise and light—the wonderful sound of her—the noise of living louder living nothing ugly a peaceful sound a peaceful noise a bird.

617. He lost it, and she—nearer, quietly human—perhaps the street, perhaps the motionless carriage—the thing from the film, a different world—a wonderful humming as the carriage stopped and the wind swept the landscape.

618. He feels in talking with his dear wife he had to hear it to hear the boy to hear Vera these would be the things to rescue him from himself his returned self.

619. Her mind now of course differed from the now of him—*no*—being is not tenable—*he went where*—he remembers it, the nagging pull at his arm—

620. 000

621. He hears it, a they—a *the dear*—and was a *is sinned*—this constant preoccupation with characterizing every facet of living, describing it, *explaining it*—

622. Joy to the world—certainly, certainly—had it what—had it clearly articulated, with I, with the Christmastime self of what—with who, with your mother, with the certain world—the case.

623. You, the you of the proverbs—the you, one was what—the workers they did so coil—the lamps, the time, the line, the noise—so howling—

624. On the street was certain death, dying—and beneath it something uglier, cancerous—**the back, the ah, the slows**—he moves upward, following the street from the hospital, he moves—

625. He is kept at ease—he is, by keeping all at ease, himself at ease—he is at the light the more—all the more he's kept at ease—the old landlady, everything compiled in the closet in a stack of—again of—his papers again of—

626. Another disaster is done when—does the water seem rotten—seen and of what—she of some ditch was they speaking there—were they heard there.

627. That it's done now is nothing it means nothing—it's something written down a proposition meaning what—it was overwhelming, the thing itself was overwhelming—growing is it—it is growing—this sense of it *it is growing, it is a mistake*—it is in fact the case.

628. But when he was a boy, the—his father never being home is what—his father present at every turn is what—when can the policeman his lighter barking—when he holds two lit cigarettes when he doesn't stop yammering outside of the house—in the winter his hand his lighter is fallen lost—*why are they watching*—

629. Piled stones suddenly in front of them this cairn this walking through the woods to see the first drips of spring from on the trees and they see this shining cairn—with his past a wretched bean this coiled thing he sought in every dumb minute he could stare upon the cairn and see no thing and want no thing and he'd been all spun out in thinking in thought and not seeing may—his not seeing may be light—

630. For them life is now for something else—something different—something close by, as their home is, as their life is—their family is—about them is clutched some presence—*come then*, he says, *late into the night*—

631. And yet away a way to die yet dying yet was off—*but what and what*, the man did think—*when and when can I die*, the man did think—on the street the man did think it with the child he did think it when—

632. Dark a curling thing a darkness a permeating darkness a total darkness a like onward darkness it feels to him like—the life of him around him fleeting out—the morning in the fog the cup of tea the route to work the boy at school—and so hoofs of what the horses what and—

633. Out together they eat in small places the canned laughter a dusk—***be more present***, he thinks to himself he wants to stop—he wants to wither he wants of what—

634. She says this some morning or some thoughts are said in morning—the light blew in they could in light bring to what—get a cab he thinks to leave the hospital he's bringing home more light—

635. She there in the dressing gown in the morning—***slowly, slowly***—there the moments could linger he walks slowly across their bedroom floor, in his slippers, and she puts her necklace on—he looks at her as she looks up at him, in the mirror, and there is peace— from all that's happened there is peace, and she looks full of every stitch of their living—

636. To whoever dimly looks about her there is peace— peace it is of herself it is her very own small thing to hold at her chest—*I have now seen how to carry on, I've figured it out, I can now carry on.*

637. They would never they would not be caught in terrible sorrowing so in the mornings over their breakfast as the cat mills from room to room they are not sorrowing—the dog is healed and she is not sorrowing he will not let himself sorrow they are indifferent to such miserabling they will open themselves yes to this living they will open not to burrowing death—

638. He thought **he must go away** these thoughts did pass over him—every day, though he considered himself a lover of life, an appreciator of his every good fortune— he did think these things—the people of the world have frightened him—*who*—*them there, the policeman there, every bureaucrat there*—*everyone and everyone more, I don't know*—he listens.

639. *She—it—life*—see the thing you seem to want— envision all that you can do, all continues to it, every stitch of it in certainty—*all*—

640. The before black in the tunneling of the accelerator is what—the quiet but persistent humming light—he does not know what anything is—what everything *was*—she must know she must in the corner of her brain hold something that light that dark it must be in there somewhere tunneling.

641. Several did speak—*and what bridge*—be raising be rising be constantly returning to the thing at hand—timing is nothing there's nothing to timing—catch any thanks you can and be generous of apology—the life the day of her and thus too we move from Moscow we move we experience life in other places on other planets other planes and the quiet doesn't stop—

642. He did warm to the notion of this being his last go around the sun—he must his body stood his presence stood within the hall again facing—his stood form his thinking grows the world is pale and gray they're meeting they're having a meeting again in the brown bar where they're outside of the Zone they're trying to converse trying to—she, she will say, she will speak and say, they will try and commune again and she will speak—

643. Unconsciously he finds himself burrowing again into his old anger again—his marital anger his sense of his life being one way and not knowing the countless other ways it might've gone—when his life seems of—of the fear his thought it hurries him it tortures him and he has returned again beneath the facility in the hospital in Moscow standing on the street looking at steam grates and feeling sick and smoking—and she is—

644. Sickness he stops it back he stands at the sink he stops it back it—she enters the cellar in winter and her going in registers and then he loses time loses hours in thought with—in thought but he cannot return he stands at the sink eating a carrot he's peeled he's— they're dining eating carrot cake he's—

645. The one in the one there occurs quite readily what and he sits staring at footage of lightning strikes—the people struck the trees struck and the strange forms on their bodies in the aftermath red trees and maps across their flesh—and, or—they are not in houses, the rainy houses again of him the burning houses in the rain the house upon the beach the small model which did—

646. Of her—would his thinking veer again back to Vera— would it could some thing get sharpened could his thinking his presence sharpen—not thing thousands of things countless things impossible things—had he a six-year stretch wherein he wore only his work uniform at every moment—

647. As a boy his vile thought of—the laziness of the fat oaf upon the bed sopping in his own rot—where we have a life isn't predetermined we have found—

648. Not man not of man he's keeping pace he's looking, watching—in the morning he watches a cartoon with the boy a man eating a pancake had hot coffee thrown in his face he flees town he runs—*terrible* the boy did laugh and whisper—*terrible* Anatol did repeat it—

649. The she in him the twinned I the you the reason his reason his raison his persisting thing the thing which—time faded shall fade wisely away, a—

650. Of the body about his body there are minimal indicators of anything having happened beyond those indicators which would—the trees the maps the doctor the woman's thinking happened to him it wasn't torpor it wasn't such torpor—was it suddenly *No*, **here**—

651. It did bridge off it veered off quite splendidly returning to its coil so of what he finally walks knowing what the knowing is—stood there he is—

652. They sent a driver but she headed out early to meet with them in her own humble car on her own humble routes and the car did eventually return—*Oh and he so very what*—more a resting, a quieting, the anxiety that year—

653. Nights the awareness did swell miserably so—as he
her sort of burden pushed on carriages he pushed their
carriage in dreams she's chasing him—*again the steps
at Odessa he's barreling in countless directions on gurneys
she's at him she's trying to she runs—*

654. Thoughts could quite wonderfully float up how peaceful
thoughts the two of them up early as Christmas came
and she—and they had felt a freedom on the farm and
a peace there away from their madnesses on—

655. Lying in bed it was early it was morning in the
morning this thing took place it's written it is writ
and thus what—in houses but under them a dim
awareness did grow as the rains fell as he sat in his
corner and she stood in her corner in their sacrifice
way an awareness dawned and the lights did burn
among those who'd come to know of the man the
doctoral candidate came to interview the man who'd
endured the torpor of the sun.

656. Thoughts might come terribly quickly and he
could mouth them curling over in their bed and

suddenly—on the light at first light she no longer slept well she was of utter fascination to their cat their dog the world at those hours—the dog did live and their driving humbly driving running errands or to work and they would—

657. The ambulances here must know him in the morning he wakens to find he's seized again and being taken and—she tells him he'd spat on one of them unwittingly a policeman and—why anybody knows anything at all again—little meandering things the moments the how it got to be suchlike and what—

658. Would hold—he cannot eat an entire apple without vomiting he cannot—and the howling the wind howling over Protvino the people howling in the street the terrible faces—seeing they have people they have sources they have reliable stable bodies to whom they can entreat—

659. The thoughts of the thought the out of being forgiven *I who ought not be forgiven and you who stood there who to me was what* and such gibberishing every middling moment the day did go and go and ponder with such pathetic academicking, *I*—

660. Now he's rendered afresh the dogs have eaten another night without what urine and we—the light the will the with—a line straight through the I from—

661. And all and the middle the line knows as the man knows on his morning on his bicycle in his woolcoat for them to be living for them to persist amid such cancer it—the nearing anywhere—

662. *Us people may some midnight quickly topple something untoward in man*—which is what—he sometimes feels buried in life, he—he crosses her path in the day's good light and whispers something to the ground as he picks up a coin.

663. Here he is in being in living of—of life it frees him he was terribly ahead from who before thought what in whatting filth—

664. Home again in morning the peaceful home the before the machines did turn on and she in mourning him away from him the light is out the I is out and she'd known and had she known—

665. The coming to work and he not ever wanting anything but what and she makes him lets him once again pummel his head down into pillows—

666. The fact of his clothes and what were his clothes— what did the man wear—his thermals his white thermals—*at this I stayed*—he hurries hours he harries noise all there all present—

667. He has—it takes him hours to figure out what— and the not, the not thinking, the moments of not

thinking—he tells his child to breathe—the stomach
hurts, the anxiety hurts the stomach—he thinks of it
of his youth and feeling terribly strange—amused and
where did—

668. *That day was like every other day except for the beam
in my head—this is what I'm communicating—it's
never been any different—it's never been different—
my life has never been any different no—for this is
not hard, this life is not hard—the physics of it I
mean—it's not difficult—I've been out in the winter,
the cold, and what—I'm done, I'm finished—
it's two in the morning—I'm tired—I'm terribly
tired—it's my—it's the eyes, I cannot stop—I
cannot stop working this way—oh I cannot—can
you open the—*

669. And has the leading of one's efforts one's thinking much changed you—she asks herself she thinks she flees in thought and he—

670. Is he somehow changed is he of wise mind afraid mind mad mind raving mind is he thinking is he—does he possess a maid are there maids do the maids help are there nurses is there a live-in nurse—he walked this plank throughout the lot and did not wonder or wish to change it.

671. Of that morning she forgot more than she now can remember and they—they—the people—the people were that right there, the body, or bodies, and the—

672. And she was pushed herself all at once all it—***do you have about you—can you suddenly***—

673. His being stands in—his being is—he is recognized as cold—his living being cold—the living in Russia then being cold—the mercy of what bestowed upon him in—few knowing anything thereto as per this fellow's what—

674. For the *there*—the question there of—thereof this question of—the there being there—this question they pose—***calmly, calmly***—she the wife of this creature now, his Vera—not having this life now of her own now—

675. About this moment in returning then to work he had to what—he had this thinking—this habit of thinking himself into—into all this missed language where is—is he with—

676. He to himself and she to herself so contentedly in living in their bed they're finally at the end of the day there upon the bed at the end of the day—and they sit with their backs to the wall in reading—articles things documents related to what—the wall does fall away she lights a cigarette in the dark and the moon is out high in the window and he smiles and they slip together as she recounts this dream—

677. Time and this country will sink the world it will sink— what and what and—but they trembled see there they did tremble the people did tremble—and he cares, sitting on the journey on the railway he **cares**—

678. Of their bodies and much time, calmly he—calmly, he—all the children have to rest—they are in bed and what—the life has slowed and the cold chill of the night doesn't touch them and the small fire did burn—

679. To this discovered premise this meeting he meets the policeman he's never particularly liked the police—his rheumatism his hands his coiling flesh it coils the same as the U-70 Synchotron, *No*—even he a person he a dead person in snow—

680. He is here he is not here I suppose he's—other than he's what—other than every other what—if the child should freeze then what—the fire burns their two bundled sets of kindling did burn the light did remind him at once—

681. As in her youth as her youth did swiftly move the river of it a boy she saw in the darkness running this horrified running these older men these canned men their stumpy flesh their oratory she did weep over him—

682. A city himself he did have the moment that moment, the—he who shivers now cold near to the bridge now he pulls his gray jacket collar to his throat to wince against the night he's home from work from talking—

683. And a place on the earth did call to him—where they'd taken the footage, the artists, moving out in circles, tracing arcs along Chernobyl—at the grounds they'd taken blocks of ice and placed them into coolers—

they'd turned them to vapor over effigies of failures—
should the water infect the doll this would—this would
give an—the thing then could have the outline—the
tracing up the fabric of the matter—not a perfect line
through Anatol's head—nor the line through the neck
of C.—it arcs, like the paths they'd walked—

684. In the air she's—the, her steps on the walks above
his office room— and her the one who what—and
her not yet his what, she the one who'd not left—the
thing given shape—the matter given resolution—the
narrative being done—

685. How with every step the world would seem to whorl—
the fat bureaucrats were making paths behind the
curtains, blue and red curtains, situating their white
collars—unharmed, the crust hears not—

686. Should what he was be—he clasps the pillow sees it the whole face his impression there the curve of his cheek the high frustrated bone—find the documents find the accounting find more to do with what—

687. She lying unconscious, he himself in what—himself unconscious they're peaceful it is finished they have ceased to live—and she shivering against who—the road from their apartment it went—the road from their home it went—

688. Lamp scolding the two of them over work—the room it scolds them in every lit thing—she soon of then, the past just there from them—some can, which frightens him—

689. There in his life on a peaceful day would he what—
then there, low to the ground—he feels it rumble—he
cannot be without her, without Vera—

690. Was there away from them was there a way—say
to their hands say darkness is going then lay down
against the earth say—*how did you find it, how did you
find out what it—how could you do that—what right
have you got—*

691. The light the light in the morning the new light did
shine on a column in the garden—it became what it
should always become the terrible reality of—life they
merrily went the life of them was—

692. Their bed and their heaven away from life—does
his corpse find hers does she—does she and then he
discover who—

693. Once to be there it was better, their work was better
and the machine was better—she the thing out there
and this did work and she of who—she of who the
novelist, she—

694. On the day when they were married her gown he held
it against him his palm against her back and—***and
had I what she***—and it seems her thinking was—her
thinking was—

695. Understand her, she who—no, whoever does—his
words she herself did hear and she did weep—she

could hold him, just hold the poor Anatol—he doesn't want this—his thinking is what—his thinking on the matter is—

696. In the wet fog of morning they walked and it was better—they, her hand in his—she, looking to the ditch beneath the bridge, to see—who, of their past life—in what cities, in what—

697. *Is there some key in this their magic* the audience would say—certainly, and the matter would be explained simply, as he understood—he, upon the road—the street, in Protvino, in the night, understood—did look up to see the same thing—the burning world, her—

698. He cannot, does not wish to distinguish in it any living rattle—his life is not so closed—in the morning the tea is warmed over—the work remains for him— the thinking, how the fog in winter—how the pond— how it's frozen now, how finally—how the light in winter reflects—how it rises—

Grant Maierhofer is the author of *Shame, Peripatet, The Compleat Lungfish, LRD*, and others. He lives in Moscow, Idaho.

Morant
Roy Goddard

bone bite snare
Michael Mc Aloran

The Face Hole
Gary J. Shipley

Dreams of Amputation
Gary J. Shipley

The Scourge of Villanie
John Marston

Civilisation: Its Cause and Cure
Edward Carpenter